WHOSE NAME
I DID NOT KNOW

Books by Chris Helvey

Purple Adobe
Whose Name I Did Not Know

Poetry

On The Boulevard

WHOSE NAME
I DID NOT KNOW

Chris Helvey

Hopewell Publications

WHOSE NAME I DID NOT KNOW
Copyright © 2013 by Chris Helvey.

Published by Hopewell
Publications, LLC
PO Box 11, Titusville, NJ
08560-0011 (609) 818-1049

info@HopePubs.com
www.HopePubs.com

International Standard Book Number: 9781933435442

Library of Congress Control Number: 2013936163

First Edition

Printed in the United States of America

For Michael, Kenton, and Clay, my three sons
with whom I am well pleased.
And for Gina.
And for Matt Ryan

Without the unflagging support, numerous readings, and always keen editorial eye of my wife Gina this book would never have been published. I also wish to express my gratitude and indebtedness to Matt Ryan, without whose encouragement I would not have cast this book upon the waters, and without whose advice and guidance it would never have become the book it grew up to be.

1

August was dying, and I didn't feel so damn fine myself.

"Let me have another Bud, Mike."

"Wanna make it a lite, champ? Noticed you've been picking up a few pounds lately."

"Most of it's muscle. I've been lifting again."

"Looks to me as if you're hoisting more beer than iron. When was the last time you had a good workout, sweat and all? April?"

I glanced out the window. An elongated afternoon was slowly being consumed by a broiling sun. The expected rains had not come and ground and sky both looked as hard as baked enamel.

"Up yours, sideways," I said, keeping my eyes on the sweltering patch of bluegrass. "Now give me my damn beer."

Mike was a decent guy; we'd gone to high school together. He'd been going to start a band; I was going to play pro ball. Only dreams, that's all our plans had been, and now some days, in the quiet hours, I could hear the broken dreams shifting in the wind.

Sitting there on the stool it struck me as strange that we'd both migrated to Lexington. Then I considered that the whole world seemed to be in a state of migration, of forever moving away from one thing and toward another. Maybe it was time for me to move to the next good country. All Kentucky seemed to give me these days was grief. At the moment I was still sober enough to resent it. Down deep an undulating level of pride remained. A couple of beers would inundate that.

The beer came down hard on the spider-webbed Formica counter and Mike stalked back over to the other end of the bar and pretended to polish it with the nasty rag he hauled around like a security blanket.

I let my eyes come back into the cool dimness of the bar. The Final Furlong was a neighborhood place off the beltway. Pictures of horses were plastered on the walls. Some were Derby winners, others had missed glory by a nose. Several were merely beautiful. I loved horse racing, even when I was too broke to bet, which, the last few years, was most of the time.

These days I struggled to keep myself in beer money. Cutting tobacco and doing odd jobs wasn't the path to riches and glory. I'd stumbled off that one long ago. For years I'd been lost in the underbrush.

The Final Furlong was dark enough so that the stains on your trousers didn't show and during the week they let you nurse a beer. I sipped and let the cool wetness slide down my throat. Then I pushed myself off the stool and strolled over to the jukebox and dialed up Bob Seger on the jukebox. I felt like a trip to "Fire Lake."

On the way back I detoured to the Men's, nodding as I went to the rest of the Thursday afternoon crowd. Didn't take much effort. Only an off-duty cop named Rigsby, who'd once let me off with a warning when I was doing 76 on New Circle Road, a dark-skinned man with a Zappa mustache, and Mrs. McLean were there. Rigsby nodded back. Mrs. McLean just stared into her Maker's Mark. She had bad teeth and worse breath and had done a lifetime's worth of staring since her husband of thirty years had died last Valentine's Day. Zappa Man was looking at something none of the rest of us could see. Bob Seger went to Fire Lake and I went and took a piss.

Things were looking up when I returned. Mike had turned on the thirteen-incher above the bar and arena football was on. Zappa Man had taken his lost, lonely gaze elsewhere, and two blondes were ensconced at a table in the back. They weren't college kids, but they were still more attractive than anyone else who'd been in the place for months. By today's standards their hair was too long and straight, but they wore tailored slacks and clean, pressed blouses, major improvements over the jeans and t-shirts favored by most of the Furlong's female clientele.

Right then I was feeling lonely and figured they might share my sentiments and welcome some company, specifically mine. So I treated myself to another beer and carried it over to their table. Who knew, maybe one of the ladies would spring for a pitcher later. If I was going to drink more beer they would have to.

"Mind if I join you?"

They hesitated, and she who hesitates is lost. I stacked the last of my coins on the peeling veneer of the small, round table and slid down onto one of two vacant chairs. Both blondes curled up their noses and looked around the room as if they'd never seen it before. That didn't bother me; I'd been ignored before.

"Hi, Frank," I said, and smiled and extended my right hand like a gentleman.

"Amber." She shook my hand softly, like she was used to shaking hands with the elderly. Blue eyes, round and shiny as new quarters, stared out of a Persian cat face.

"Denise." All I got was fingertips, as if she was trying to avoid contamination. Her eyes were dark, half-closed as though she really didn't want to look at me.

Irritation rose in my throat. I had a few feelings left, bruised and battered, but my own. I swallowed the irritation. Irritation is a luxury lonely men can't afford.

"You ladies from Lexington?"

"No, Paris." Blue eyes was the designated speaker.

"Oh, Bourbon County."

"Yeah, that's right. You been there before?"

"Actually, I get up there quite often. I'm in the tobacco business." I didn't tell them which end of the tobacco business.

They might think I was a wealthy tobacco farmer or prosperous cigarette manufacturing executive. So what? For all I knew they might be affluent Bluegrass matrons out slumming. I didn't think so; their clothes and watches were straight out of the mall, but you never knew. Anyway, I wasn't a snob, more a cynical realist. A long fall from glory will turn a man that way.

I put both hands on the table, palms down, so they could see what fine, rugged hands I had, and that I wasn't wearing a ring. Neither Amber nor Denise seemed interested in my manly hands, so I put the left one in my lap and picked up my beer with my right. Conversation wasn't exactly flowing, so I took a sip to lubricate my tongue and energize my brain.

"Nice weather we've been having."

Denise rolled her eyes as if weather talk offended her sensibilities. "Too hot," was Amber's reply.

I took another sip of beer and reconnoitered. The chemistry wasn't great, but the night wasn't over either. Plus, if any of my cohorts strolled in they would see Frank Kohler sitting with two hot babes, just like in the old college glory days.

Actually, Amber needed a nose job and Denise had buck teeth to go with her weak chin, but they had nice bodies, wore their clothes tight, and were, far and away, the finest ladies I'd been within months.

I wished I could buy them a drink. Hell, I wished I could buy me a drink. Buying drinks for ladies always warmed the atmosphere and made them feel they owed you a little something, even if it was only pleasant conversation. I stared at the table top. A short stack of coins was not going to raise the temperature even one degree.

Amber and Denise developed a sudden interest in arena football. Silence wrapped itself around the table like a boa constrictor. I downed my beer in long, slow swallows while the ladies sipped on strawberry daiquiris. Everyone was having one hell of a fine time being bored out of their mind.

About six, the girls exchanged a glance even a drunk could recognize as meaningful, examined their powdered faces in the mirrors of their compacts, and stood up. Phony smiles stretched like cheap elastic across their faces. Amber cleared her throat.

"Nice to meet you, Greg, but we have to go now."

"It's Frank," I said, giving them my touchdown smile.

"Oh, sorry, Frank, that's right." Amber shifted her weight from one leg to another like a nervous filly. "Well, we'd better be going."

I summoned up the dregs of my courage. "Yeah, it's not really jumping in here tonight. Might as well go myself." Acting as though I'd just hatched a great idea, I leaned closer to the blondes. "Say, you two want some company?"

Pure terror flickered across Denise's face, pulling back her upper lip to reveal large, horsy teeth. She really needed to avoid that pose.

Amber started walking toward the door. "Not tonight, Greg, we're meeting friends."

"Wait a second and I'll walk you to your car. Headed that way anyway."

Surprisingly, they halted. Anything to avoid a scene, I figured as I chugged the last inch and a half of beer. It was warm and flat, but the cornerstone of my current philosophy of life was never waste alcohol in any form. I maneuvered myself between the blondes and the three of us walked across the floor like we owned it. I gave Mike the high sign, held the door, and smiled to myself as two Bourbon County beauties and one aging ex-fullback stepped into the night.

I walked them through the warm darkness to their car and held their doors for them, like the true Southern Gentleman I once aspired to be. Smiling and waving casually, I watched them speed out of the parking lot. For all they knew I had people to meet and places to go and a new BMW to transport me. I hoped they remembered old Frank Kohler fondly. Paths had a way of separating only to intersect down the line.

When all I could see was their taillights I gave it up and started the long walk home. It was too early to quit, but I was flat broke. Anyway, I needed to get back in shape. More exercise and less beer sounded like a good program, so I began humping down Menifee. At the Crofton intersection I cut through the vacant lot where the Texaco station had been before it burned, hopped the chain-link fence behind K-Mart and angled across their nearly empty parking lot.

I was making irregular payments on a stucco bungalow on Culpepper that I'd signed for in more prosperous times. Star Bank held the mortgage, and their latest letter indicated that they were not particularly pleased with my hit-and-miss payment plan. The place needed fresh stucco and the yard hadn't been mowed in three weeks, but it was home.

Scraggly weeds and dried-up grass put up only token resistance as I marched across. The porch light had burned out and nobody was waiting for me on the far side of a wooden door desperately needing paint. That was alright; I'd been letting myself in for years.

It was comforting to hear the door click shut against the world. Granted, the old home-place needed airing and a major cleaning, but the television worked and I had a half-pint hidden away beneath my black socks for just such a night.

I retrieved it, tossed the yellowing newspaper out of my cracked vinyl Lazy Boy, and spent a quiet evening with my friend Jack Daniels watching black and white movies on TCM. Their stark simplicity addressed some need drifting below the surface of my mind. Maybe it was because they presented life the way I always wanted it to be.

Jack didn't mind if the films were dated. He and I had spent many such evenings together. Over the years, we'd discovered that we liked each other's company, regardless of what images flickered before us.

2

Sunlight slipped in through the missing slats of the Venetian blinds and entered my bedroom uninvited, about half a century too early. I had a head that felt like Nebraska gone bad and my stomach rolled and pitched like the North Atlantic tossed by a late season hurricane.

For a very long time I simply lay very still. Gradually the waves of nausea began to flatten out. The cracking going on inside my skull subsided and I began to be able to see and hear again. I told myself I was never going to drink that much again. Then again, a man who'd lie before he gets out of bed in the morning will lie the rest of the day, too.

Traffic was light on Culpepper, and I lay there listing to what passed, trying to decide if I wanted to live. By noon I finally felt well enough to levitate myself off the bed and stumble to the window. My abs were sore and my legs didn't want to work properly. I hadn't shaved in three days, and my breath was sour in my mouth. I'd slept in my clothes and seemed to have lost my watch. Even the hair on the top of my head hurt. I wished I could remember the night before. I didn't recall being in a fight, but images of falling flickered at the edges.

I leaned my elbows on the dirty windowsill and watched the world go by. Slowly a new sensation began to settle across my stomach. Amazingly, I was beginning to get hungry. I gave up watching the world and went to see what culinary delights awaited.

Slim Pickens was a name of a character actor I remembered from movies gone by; the two words also described the current state of my larder. My half loaf of Kroger multi-grain bread had developed mold, I was out of hot dogs and bologna, and my sole banana resembled a mushy, shriveled black penis.

I did find a handful of half-stale Cheerios, but my milk was a week out of date. No crackers, canned goods, or candy bars, but, miracle of miracles, on the third shelf next to the toaster that only worked on one side and had been the solitary departing gift from a woman with whom I had once shared a different life, was a jar of instant Maxwell House.

It felt suspiciously light when I picked it up, but that day the gods were generous. Enough dirty brown powder remained to make at least two cups. I rinsed out the Federated Investors cup I'd scarfed from my broker, back when I'd had a broker, and fired the microwave up.

That coffee tasted like the drink of the gods. I drank the first cup so fast it scalded my tongue, washing down a couple of handfuls of aging Cheerios along the way. I lingered at the kitchen counter over the second cup.

Until April, I'd always sipped my coffee while sitting down at my kitchen table. On April Fool's Day I'd sold it to my neighbor Mrs. Curry for fifteen dollars and a homemade apple pie. I always seemed to need cash and food, and never had been too hard on the young man in the Bible who had sold his birthright for a mess of porridge.

After that second cup of coffee and a long hot shower, followed by a very short cold one, I began to feel human. As I dressed in my cleanest dirty shirt I took stock of my financial situation.

A thorough search of pants pockets, dresser drawers, and assorted hiding places turned up two quarters, an ancient Roosevelt dime, and four pennies. Sixty-four cents to my name wasn't overly promising. I'd closed my checking account last July, and hadn't had a savings account in years. Reality dictated I find employment.

Jobs were available in the tobacco fields. But who in the hell wanted to sweat to death before they were forty? Not this old boy. August in the Ohio Valley is a moist wool blanket, saran-wrapped to your skin in ninety degree temperatures. I'd had enough of that when I wore helmets and pads and packed a pigskin. Ancient I'm not, but these days my knees ache if I bend too much, I'm packing twenty extra pounds around the middle, and my motivation has gone south.

Still, I had to find employment, and with the weekend coming up, if I wanted to party, it had better include payment in cash. Actually, it wasn't so much that I wanted to party, more that I could feel all four walls closing in. I slugged back the last of my coffee and headed for the door. I wasn't sure where I was going; figured I'd know it when I got there.

Turning right at the sidewalk, I strolled down Culpepper. With a soft breeze in my face I played around with the idea of swinging by Jerry's and lifting weights. Jerry was a good enough neighbor. He liked to pump iron, drink beer, and watch college football. Plus, he was probably good for a twenty till payday. But I already owed him thirty-five. I kept walking. Thirty minutes later and two miles south I curled left on Thomas just east of the Carnegie Center and remembered Mrs. Hopkins.

Anna Hopkins was a short, fat, sweet lady who had lost her husband but kept her very large yard. It was uneven ground, spotted with old, dark trees, whose roots wormed their way along the ground, and sprinkled with a haphazard assortment of shrubs that hadn't been trimmed in years. One forsythia had to be at least ten feet tall. Anna mostly stayed in the house these days. Fallen tree limbs and windblown brush dotted her yard. Not an easy yard to mow, but she was good for twenty bucks. Thank God and Roosevelt for social security.

I hustled on over to Woodcrest. Half a block away I could see the grass, tall and twisted and tangled. Mrs. Hopkins was home. Already, I could hear her television.

An hour and a half later I was pushing the decrepit mower around the last lap. My shirt was off and sweat ran down my face like rainwater. Every muscle in my legs ached and my throat was sandpaper.

As the motor died, I heard someone calling my name.

"Mr. Kohler, Mr. Kohler."

"What?"

"Would you like something cold to drink?"

"Sure." I pushed the mower toward a shed tilting to port behind the house, half hidden by an ancient maple that sheltered a family of dark-winged birds. The oil-spattered motor popped and cracked as it cooled and all four tires wobbled. I empathized.

Her hair was lint gray and she sagged and bulged in places most people didn't have places, but her face was bisected by an honest smile and lights sparkled in her faded blue eyes.

"Lemonade, or iced tea, Mr. Kohler? The lemonade is fresh."

A beer was what I wanted. "Lemonade, please," is what I said.

"I'm so glad you came today. The yard was looking awful and help is so hard to get. Since I broke my hip last winter I don't get out much, but I do enjoy looking out the window at the birds and the sunshine."

"Plenty of sunshine, that's for sure." I stepped across the wooden floor and intercepted Mrs. Hopkins on her way back from the kitchen. She used a walker now and her jerky passage caused the lemonade to slosh dangerously near the rim of the green glass.

"Don't know about birds though. Do you have many?"

"Oh, my yes. Just let me sit down and I'll tell you all about them." She separated herself from the walker and eased onto an overstuffed brown chair dotted with dark, irregular stains. I wondered how she ever got up.

"Let's see now," she said, pursing her lips and rubbing the palm of her left hand across a deeply lined cheek. "I have robins and cardinals and catbirds and thrushes and several different kinds of finches. Then there are always sparrows and starlings, but I don't really count those. Oh, and a mockingbird. He sings in the mimosa almost every evening. My birds just love all the trees and bushes in the yard. They provide them shelter and refuge and places to build their nests and raise their families. Do you like birds, Mr. Kohler?"

"Sure," I said. I raised my glass. The lemonade was tart enough to constrict my throat. Mrs. Hopkins must have rationed the sugar, or perhaps she simply forgot. When I could speak again, I said, "Hawks are my favorite."

Mrs. Hopkins clapped her hands together like a pleased child. "Oh, good, hawks were Mr. Hopkins' favorite, too. He used to sit in that old rocker next to you and talk for hours about retiring from the paper and going out west and becoming involved in falconry." She sighed and the lights dimmed in her eyes. "Dreams, only dreams, Mr. Kohler. All he ever had were his dreams. He died too soon."

I sipped at the lemonade. "Sometimes dying too soon is better than dying too late." Sucking on an ice cube I'd secured only after a struggle, I asked, "Didn't he work for the *Herald Leader*?"

"Yes, he was a writer. Fourteen years. Before that twelve with the *Corbin Daily Tribune*."

"Business? Sports? Editorials?"

"Sports. He loved his Wildcats."

I smiled and put my lemonade down on a lacy doily the color of old snow. I walked across the room and patted Mrs. Hopkins' bare forearm. The flesh was soft as pudding and age spots marched in uneven ranks toward her shoulder. "Good for him. It was after his tenure, but I played a little football for Kentucky."

She lifted her face toward mine. I felt her slip money into my hand. "I know, Mr. Kohler. I've followed you since your days at Frankfort High. You always seemed like such a nice boy, and at Murray my roommate's last name was Kohler. Also, you spoke nicely when you and those other Christian Athletes came to our church. Always had a soft spot in my heart for you, even when you've had tough times. I pray for you every day, you, and all my boys. Would you like to pray together, now?"

Inside my skin I shivered. It was unnerving having the old woman pray for me. Never realized I was anybody to her except the yard man. All that unrequited caring was more than I could handle. I bent down and kissed her furrowed forehead. She smelled like fading flowers.

"Not right now, I've got an appointment. But you go ahead and pray for me anytime. I need it."

She patted at my arm. "We all need prayer, Mr. Kohler. You run along now. Show your good manners by being on time."

I left her sitting. A wisp of gray hair had fallen across her forehead and the lights in her eyes had turned inward. A sad smile played at the corners of her mouth. All the way back to Thomas Street I wondered what she was remembering. Crossing Thomas I began to remember what I was trying to forget.

Halfway home, I realized that if I drifted west a couple of blocks I would go by Ralph Adams' place.

Ralph was a huge fan of University of Kentucky football. He'd been following the Wildcats since the days of his youth at the head of Briar Creek in Whitley County. During my years on campus he'd been an active booster. Since then, he'd endured a pair of heart attacks. These days he followed the 'Cats on radio or television. Still, for an ex-Wildcat fullback he was always good for a couple of cold beers. I took Horace Greeley's advice.

The sun was low-riding on the western horizon now, drifting behind the tallest of the trees lining the sidewalk. Lengthening shadows migrated to the middle of the street, then slipped across the yellow line. Blatant afternoon heat had given way to muggy afterglow. My shirt was plastered to my back and my throat felt as dry as the Sonoran Desert. I hoped Ralph was home; I hadn't walked a mile out of my way for my health.

A block away I could hear his radio. It was turned to a sports talk show on WVLK. Three houses away I could see him sitting in the deep shade of his front porch. Slowing to a saunter, I sucked in my stomach. Just an ex-athlete out for an evening stroll.

Ralph got out of his chair as I crossed the street. By the time I'd made his porch steps he was there to greet me, smiling.

"Well, look at what wandered in. If it ain't that old Wildcat from yesteryear, Frank Kohler." He stuck out his right hand. He had a beer can in his left. "Number 33, wasn't it?"

"That's right, Ralph." I shook his hand. It was bigger than mine and his grip was still strong, although not the bone-crusher I remembered. "How you doing?"

"Not bad for an old man. How about yourself?"

"Fine."

"Got time to sit a spell?" He jerked his head toward the porch. I looked up Powell Street like I had somewhere to be.

"A few minutes," I said.

"Want a beer?" He waggled his can of Bud at me.

"Sounds good."

"Come up and grab a seat while I get you a cold one."

He turned and walked stiffly across the porch, moving like all his joints were hurting. Climbing the stairs, I realized that my joints were aching. I wondered how long it would be until I looked old.

Purple shadows stretched until they parted at the seams and began to bleed black. We sat on the porch in that quiet, easy ways guys have, not talking, only sipping cold beer and watching the death throes of another day. Fireflies began to flicker on and off and unseen birds rustled themselves to sleep.

Ralph broke the silence. "Been over to watch the Cats practice?"

"Couple of times."

"They look any good?"

I sipped at my beer. "Got some speed; not much size on the line though."

Ralph cleared his throat and spat into the yard. "Always been tough for Kentucky to compete with the big names, north and south. North of here, the hoss linemen go to Ohio State, or Michigan, or Notre Dame. South, they go to Florida, or Georgia, or Tennessee."

"We get some good ones."

"Not enough."

"We went to three bowls when I was in school," I said.

Ralph snorted. "Yeah, and two of them so small that nobody cared. Hell, Frank, one of 'em ain't even still around."

"What about my senior year? Remember the Peach Bowl?"

"Sure, and the only reason you went is because you and the boys in the line were all seniors and knew the game and blocked so well that Marshall had some huge days against the wannabes and made a name for himself."

"Over two hundred yards rushing against Louisville and Indiana wasn't shabby."

Ralph Adams shifted in his chair. "You're still blocking for him, Frank. Indiana only won two games that year, and Louisville lost to every non-conference team they played."

"Ralph, Preston Marshall was an All-American, first team, and a finalist for the Heisman trophy."

"Sure. Don't get me wrong. I'm not saying the man didn't have talent. But check the records. All his big games came against soft competition. Ran a punt back all the way against Northern Illinois, took a kickoff one hundred yards against Navy, and four touchdowns against Vanderbilt—all of them in the second half after you all were already ahead by fourteen."

I swallowed my anger and some more beer. "Preston had two touchdowns in the Peach Bowl."

The old man stood up and went over and leaned against a faded white column. "Right, and both were late in the fourth quarter against the second string."

"What about that seventy-seven yard touchdown reception against Georgia? They were a top ten team all year."

"True," Ralph said. "But, as I recall, they were blitzing and he was ten yards behind the defense. All he had to do was catch the ball and turn on the afterburners. With his speed, nobody was going to catch him."

"He was a very fast man," I said by way of agreement, and hit the beer again.

"Was, and still is."

"What do you mean by that, Ralph?"

The old man tilted his can back and took a long swallow. Streetlights had arced on and light reflected off aluminum. The wattle below his chin wobbled as he drank.

"I don't mean anything, except that Preston Marshall was, and is, a mover and a groover. Know he was your roommate and best pal, and all that stuff back when you were both big men on campus, and I don't aim to hack you off, but—"

"But what?"

"But nothing, really. I've still got contacts, you know. They talk and I listen. Hear lots of things that way."

He arched his eyebrows, making himself look like one of the late Roman emperors. "Now it's just my opinion, and that and a dollar bill will get you a coffee at McDonalds, that old Preston's best skill was always getting a really good man to run interference for him. He was a good thinker, I'll give him that. Had a knack for seeing the field in front of him, knowing how he wanted the play to develop, then directing it that way."

"Ralph, you're getting crazier by the day. Go and get us another beer."

The old man looked directly into my eyes for a minute. Then he gave me a lopsided grin I couldn't decipher, turned and walked back across the porch. I pushed myself out of my chair and eased down the steps and into the yard.

It was pleasant to stand in the yard full of purple shadows and the first flickering fireflies and the last birds calling sleepily to each other. It was cooler now, with that soft summertime edge to the air, and that good beer taste was still in my mouth and the memories flowed like water from the Triangle Park fountain.

I remembered graduation day and how my future seemed so bright that it had hurt my eyes to gaze at it. Success was hanging out there, just like a ripe peach on a low limb. All I had to do was reach up and pluck it. Where had that sweet fruit gone?

Dark grew thick around me as I tried to puzzle out where it had all gone wrong. A man takes so many steps over a lifetime it's hard to say which one took him off the trail.

Things had started to slide after the Peach Bowl. Studies and workouts had been supplanted by sex and alcohol. Still, it was hard to believe those things were so terrible. Frustration with myself and life filled my mind and made it ache. I was glad to hear footsteps behind me on the dampening grass.

3

Downtown, the buildings were tall and wide and blocked the sunlight from the pavement. Shadows ran thick and deep and dark. Even in August it was cool in the shadows, and I slowed, savoring the relief.

Saturday afternoons tend to be slow in Lexington, especially in the late summer before the students return to campus and football starts. The humidity was up today, and the announcer on WVLK said the temperature was ninety-three at Bluegrass Airport. Deep in the concrete and asphalt jungle it had to be several degrees hotter. Hated to think what the heat index would reach. You had to really want to go someplace to venture out.

I really wanted a cold one at Grant's. I had beer at home, well a couple, but I was fresh out of frosted mugs. Besides, Grant's usually had air conditioning. I had a ten-year-old oscillating Sears desk fan.

Grant's was a small bar that had begun life as a candy store. To get to Grant's I had to walk through the dozen or so blocks that comprise downtown Lexington, what's left of it. The Final Furlong would have been closer, but I still owed Mike money.

Saturday afternoon, and the once bustling center of Lexington was as empty as a plundered pharaoh's tomb. Never saw another pedestrian as I trekked deserted sidewalks. The air seemed saturated with a heavy quiet. Newspapers rustled in the hot wind and two gray and white pigeons cooed at each other beneath a rotting overhang. Except for the few cars rolling by on their way to some other place, it was like walking through a city whose population had been wiped out by a cataclysmic event. By the time I reached Grant's I had a full blown case of the creeps. I needed a drink more than ever.

Grant's was a downtown sort of place, not redneck, but not a yuppie bar either. More a gathering place for those of us who didn't follow trends, who were lonely and had lost our way, who needed a safe place.

The bricks that formed the outside of Grant's had been painted over so many times that no one remembered their original color. Faded mustard was the current rendition. Where the paint was flecking, parrot green gleamed through. The corners of the building were chipped and a large crack bisected the left side of the bar's façade two feet above the sidewalk.

An ugly building, but the beer was cold, nobody cared who you were or what you looked like, and you could usually cage a drink. I pulled out my semi-clean handkerchief, mopped at the sweat standing at attention on my forehead, and pushed the door open.

Darkness greeted me, along with cooler air, the voice of Bruce Springsteen, and pungent odors of stale cigarette smoke, human sweat, stagnant beer and a dozen other components I was afraid to identify.

Nobody spoke, but that was okay. It wasn't a place to make lifelong friends. Conversations generally centered on horse racing, ball games, politics, vehicles, and the rising cost of living. Grant's was not where you confessed sins, closed a deal, or discussed Aristotelian logic.

At Grant's you might pick up a lady, down on her luck and a little worn around the edges, for a one-night stand. You wouldn't want to meet your future bride there.

Just inside the door I paused and let my eyes adjust to the dim lighting. Ancient ceiling fans stirred cool musty air around, while above the bar a television set broadcast the Reds game. They were in third place and, like most of the regulars at Grant's, going no place fast.

Counting the bartender and two cocktail waitresses, there might have been twenty people in the bar. I knew the staff, one of the two guys shooting pool, and two or three of the desperados lined up at the bar. The desperados were all sitting on cracked red leatherette seats, eyes glued to the tube, nursing beers and memories.

There was a very tall, very thin man standing quietly at the bar. He had a face like an axe blade, sharp and pointed and hard, that I'd seen somewhere before. Perhaps on television, or at the Keeneland Spring

Meet. Didn't really know him. The rest of the patrons I'd never seen before, not the couples staring deeply into each other's eyes, not the predators on the prowl laughing at their own desperate humor, not the lonely staring with expressionless eyes over beers into a future that held no golden promises.

The men I knew were quite likely to be as nearly broke as I was and I'd learned years ago the futility of casting my fate on the mercy of strangers. There were only enough ones in my pocket to help me make it through a careful hour. Keeping them in reserve, I decided to provide hatchet face with an opportunity to buy his old acquaintance a drink. Smoothing my hair back with my hands, I fixed my best Saturday afternoon special smile on my face and started meandering his way.

Two hours later I was reasonably polluted, and damn near broke. I had talked hatchet face out of a double Knob Creek. Halfway to the bar, he'd turned his head, and I'd recognized him as the trainer of Equanimity who had won the Lexmark Stakes a couple of years ago. After he left, I scored a beer off the service manager of Don Jacob's Honda, who had been a year behind me at Kentucky. Then I'd bought myself another.

The Reds were down by four in the bottom of the eighth and I was down to two dollars when I felt a hand drop heavily onto my left shoulder.

I studied the hand. On the ring finger of the man's right hand was a Peach Bowl ring I recognized instantly. It was from my senior year. For years, I'd owned one exactly like it. Then I'd run out of luck and money in Atlanta and had traded my ring to a genuine Cats fan for a Greyhound ticket to Lexington. Not sure I wanted to know, I looked up to see who was wearing the ring. Some people belong in the past.

Funny how in just an instant all the memories are there. Of course, when you wake up for the biggest part of four years in the same room with a guy he makes a rather permanent impression on you. I slid off my stool and stuck out my hand.

"Preston Marshall, as I live and breathe."

"Frank Kohler, good to see you." Press put out his own right hand and shook mine. He was slim and tanned and his grip was firm. There were no calluses on the palms of his hands.

"How's it going, Press?"

"Great, roomie, and with you?"

"Making it."

Preston flashed two rows of even, white teeth and jerked his head toward the door. "Hey, Frank, you remember Les."

My eyes followed his lead. Instantly, I knew his question was rhetorical. You didn't forget a man who is six and a half feet tall, weighs close to three hundred pounds, and is as black as the bowels of Mammoth Cave.

"Les Johnson, you old son-of-a-bitch."

"Frank, my man. Been a while." Les stepped out of the smoky shadows and shook my hand. I'm not a small man and my hands are big for my size, but mine was engulfed by his. He hadn't lost any of the strength that made him a two-time, first string, all SEC lineman. He still had calluses.

"What are you two up to? Slumming?"

"No way. Just on our way to a meeting," Preston said.

I studied their dark suits and neatly patterned ties. Press was wearing what looked like an Armani. Their shoes shone and their cologne smelled good.

"Don't tell me you stopped by Grant's for a draft."

Press chuckled. "No, we didn't stop in for a drink. We're a little short on time. Matter of fact, we're already late. What we were really doing, Frank, was looking for you."

"For me?"

"Absolutely." Press patted me on the shoulder. "I'm throwing a party next weekend, an expanded reunion of the Peach Bowl team, and over the years I'd misplaced your address. Les heard Grant's was one of your hangouts and it was on our way."

To give me a few seconds to think I took a sip of my beer. Successes like Preston Marshall didn't frequent Grant's.

"What sort of party?" I asked. "Black tie? I don't own a tuxedo."

"No, just a little get-together at my place. Next Saturday night. Can you make it?"

"I'll check my calendar. But I don't have your address either."

"Not a problem. It'll be on the invitation." Press took a small leather notebook out of an inside coat pocket. His suit was an Armani.

"Let me get your address. Hate to rush after all the years, but I should have been someplace else ten minutes ago." He gave me a *GQ* smile.

I gave him my address and walked them to the door. For the length of time it took to cross the beer-stained floor it was old times. We shook hands again and I opened the door. They stepped with purpose into the hot night. A cream-colored Benz was idling at the curb. A man whose face I couldn't see sat behind the wheel.

"Thanks for coming," I said to their retreating backs.

They waved and Les held the back door for Press. I went back inside and finished my beer. As I drank thoughts flickered like heat lightning. None made sense. All they gave me was a vague sense of uneasiness and a headache. To ease the pain I ordered another beer. My last for the night. I was out of cash.

4

The invitation came. I would have enjoyed witnessing the expression on the postman's face. My mail usually consisted of past-due bills, circulars, and requests from worthy causes who had yet to appreciate how truly needy I was. If they had better understood the situation they would have sent me a donation.

I sucked it up and went out and found work. Mowed a lawn on Crestview, helped unload trucks at Furniture World, did after-hours floor mopping for a buddy who ran a janitorial service. The work I found was hot, hard, and significantly lacking in glamour, but not ignoble.

I stayed reasonably sober all week, lifted weights twice with Jerry, and even jogged a couple of miles. Felt positively virtuous.

All my efforts paid off with enough cash to get my only suit pressed and my hair cut. I bought a brand new white shirt at Sears and bummed a stain-free tie off Jerry. There was enough left over to fund a cab ride to Preston's place on Saturday night. Granted, there was only a dollar to tip the cabbie, but he'd been a touch surly anyway.

Nearly an hour late, but showered and cologned, I stood at the bottom of Preston Marshall's driveway. It wound up a long hill like a humongous snake, black and curving and shining where yard lights reflected on the asphalt.

An imposing castle loomed at the end of the drive. Jags, Caddies, Benz, and a Lexus or two were parked in neat rows. Swallowing the self-pity that was welling up in my throat, I walked up the drive trying to pretend I owned the place.

The action was around back. You could hear the party well before you could see it. Angling across the lawn, I worked my way around the house. The grass was like plush carpet and the house more massive than it had appeared at the foot of the drive. For a halfback, Preston Marshall had done damn well.

The party was a catered affair. White jacketed waiters wandered among the throng, balancing trays of drinks and hors d'oeuvres. Long tables, covered with white linen sagged beneath warming trays of food, massive floral arrangements, and stacks of plates and glasses. A bar, complete with two barmen, was set up by a swimming pool.

I couldn't locate Preston or Les in the swirling mass, so I wandered over and had one of the barmen draw me a beer. The man was about my height with a dark complexion and a bushy mustache. He was more friendly than my cab driver, but then Preston was probably paying him better.

Wandering, I caught snippets of conversation. A man whose stomach hung over his belt was talking about a piece of property he'd just purchased outside Orlando to an extraordinarily tall man whose face I'd once seen on television. A thirty-something brunette was earnestly instructing a blonde about financially effective divorce procedures. The brunette was virtually hipless. The blonde's creamy breasts were nearly exposed by her low-cut gown, and her eyes were fixed on the brunette's face. Two youngish men in light-colored suits stood centurion erect under the floodlights. They sipped at martinis and spoke in reverent tones about a bull market, and less enthusiastically about a pharmaceutical stock whose name I vaguely recognized.

A few famous people were scattered among the two hundred or so meandering across the lawn, as well as a few nearly famous that I'd met over the years, but no one I really knew. So I drifted back to the bar and had the man with the mustache draw me another beer. Then I worked my way through the crowd and up a grassy slope.

At the top of the hill, trees ran in a straight line across a smooth expanse of grass. They were tall and thickly leaved and it was notice-ably darker beneath their branches. I sat down with my back against the trunk of one and watched the crowd mill about below. Sipping beer, I was struck rather forcibly by a fragmentary line from an old song by Credence Clearwater Revival, "happy creatures dancing on the lawn."

A cool breeze had sprung up and it was pleasant sitting with my back against the tree. Conversations of the partygoers merged into a soothing babble and the beer was cold. Wind and dark and solitude suited me.

I sat at the top of the hill and drank my beer as I watched other people wander up the hill and go down again. No one noticed me.

A couple came up the hill hand-in-hand. In the shelter of the shadows they embraced, then kissed. She murmured and he answered her back, but their words were spoken too softly for me to understand. One man toiled slowly up the hill, then urinated deep in the dark shadows. I wanted another beer, but not enough to abandon my splendid dark solitude.

I thought about some unsatisfying choices I'd made over the years and watched a couple climbing the slope. They were headed in my general direction. Something in the man's walk struck me as familiar. Twenty yards out I recognized Preston. I didn't know the woman until she spoke.

"So there you are, Frank. Remember me?"

"Sure. How are you Beth?" I really did remember her, and I should have. After all, I'd been best man at their wedding. Even fifteen years and twenty-five pounds were not sufficient disguises.

"Oh, I'm fine, very fine. And you? Are you okay?"

"I'm fine, too. Why wouldn't I be?"

She took a quick sip the glass in her right hand. "Because you're way up here all by yourself. We saw you come in, but we were talking to Judge Chandler and he just wouldn't shut up. Then you got lost in the crowd. Press and I have been searching ever since."

Preston stepped forward and patted my shoulder. He wasn't carrying a drink. "Yeah, buddy, what in the world are you doing way up here in the dark all by your lonesome?"

"Not much of anything, "I replied. "Just sitting, and sipping, and surveying."

They turned their heads in unison and stared down the slope. Partygoers looked like midgets scurrying about to an internal rhythm. Strands of lights glittered like ribbons of low hanging stars. Even the huge house seemed in some way diminished.

"Quite a view from here," Preston said. "Should get up here more often."

"Don't kid yourself. You're hardly ever home. Too busy, certainly too busy to tour the estate. Always working, or a meeting or a dinner to go to. Too busy for me." Beth sniffed and took another drink.

"I was home Tuesday night, all night."

"Exactly."

"What do you mean, exactly?" Press asked.

"I mean one night this week. You've been home one night this week."

"What about tonight?"

"Tonight doesn't count."

"And why not?"

"Because it's a party. You're here for the party."

Preston put a hand on Beth's bare back and began rubbing. "Not true, not totally. Sure there's a party, but I'm also here because you're here."

"Really?" Beth asked.

Sad to hear so much hope and pleasure contained in a single word. I needed another drink.

Preston kissed her lightly. "Really. Now, I have to go back down and hook up with some people. Just before we began our trek I saw the mayor and her husband, so I need to go and say my hellos. You two stay here and chat about old times."

He bent forward and stuck out his right hand. "Thanks for coming, Frank." Preston leaned closer and whispered in my ear. "Keep an eye on Beth for me. She's a touch high."

"Sure," I said.

"Thanks, roomie," he said. Then he gave Beth a quick peck on the lips, and both of us a wave as he started back down the hill. His back was straight and he moved with purpose.

I watched him until I felt Beth's hand on my arm.

"Frank, may I join you?"

"Sure." I held her drink as she eased her body to the grass. It was a tall glass, nearly full of what I figured was whiskey. As she maneuvered into position I noticed the push of her stomach against her dress. Beth had always been a touch chunky, but being a cheerleader and working out had kept her in decent shape. Apparently she had given up on the workouts and taken up eating, or drinking, or both. A couple of belly rolls provided evidence.

"How long has it been?" she asked.

"Quite a while." I handed her back her glass.

"Funny how we used to spend so much time together, double dates even, and now we've just drifted apart." Beth sipped at her drink and eyed me over the top of the glass. Her eyes were exactly as I remembered and her lips unchanged. Excess flesh distorted the rest of her face.

"The world just keeps spinning."

"And we don't?" Beth asked.

"Different orbits," I said.

"You married, Frank?"

"Never."

"Why not?"

"No one would have me."

Beth laughed. "Poor baby."

"Life is tough."

"And so are you," Beth said.

"Tough enough," I said, not listing what I was tough enough for.

Beth nodded and took another sip. I borrowed her glass and joined her. We didn't talk much, just a word or two now and then. Mostly we sipped and watched stars illuminate the blackness. The evening slid through our fingers like warm, perfumed water. When her glass was empty I helped her up and we started back down the hill. She began telling me a story about her mother's fears. A lot of memories were jostling for position and my head was beginning to hurt; I only pretended to listen as I watched the people grow larger and their features become more delineated.

Beth babbled beside me as we descended. In my condition it was simply too tough to concentrate on both walking and listening. So I focused on putting one foot safely in front of the other. I wasn't drunk yet, but the buzz was starting and I was anxious to get there. Besides, I wasn't really interested in what she had to say. The story about her mother had evolved into a feminine philosophy about the appeal of certain men and certain food. All the words merged until I became slightly nauseous. Every few steps I smiled and nodded at her. After all, she was Preston's wife.

All the time we were walking I was wondering why Preston had really invited me. A factor of the equation was missing. That missing symbol buzzed around my head like a lethargic wasp.

If she caught on to my duplicity Beth never let it show. She just kept talking and walking. The ground began to level out and small tables full of hors d'oeuvres and dessert pastries appeared. Beth seemed to have never met a smoked sausage, egg roll, or cheese ball she didn't like. Without paying any particular attention, I watched her eat. Easy to see how she'd picked up those extra pounds. I began to look for her husband, or a good excuse to leave her side.

I found the bartender and switched to whiskey. Getting to be that sort of night. It was already that sort of life.

A five-piece combo had set up on the heart shaped patio that butted up against the pool. They completed their warm up and started getting serious. On the far side of the band a redhead in something green and shimmery who looked worth knowing swayed to the rhythm. In another life I'd been a decent dancer.

Beth was still standing beside me. Inside my mind the redhead was smiling at me. "Think I'll drift over and listen to the band. Good to see you again."

That wasn't a lie; I was glad to have seen her again. However, I'd performed my penance, at least according to my religion.

She licked barbecue sauce off her fingers before she gave me her hand. Her skin felt soft and sticky. "Okay," she said, a smile playing peek-a-boo on her lips, "and it was good to see you, too, Frank. Don't be such a stranger."

I waved back at her over the top of my head as I headed toward the band, the pool, and the redhead. Beth was a sweet lady but she needed to lose thirty pounds and cut back on the drinking. I took another sip of my drink and realized I could stand to follow my own advice.

Night settled dark and heavy on my shoulders. The beat of the drum reverberated against the walls of my mind.

I awoke and I was blind.

I blinked and the blindness dissipated enough to let me discover that it was only full morning sunlight striking me open-handed across the face. I glanced down and away from the glare in an effort to discover where I was. Waking up and not knowing where you were was unnerving.

Seemed that I'd spent the night at Preston's house. Actually, I'd passed out in, or been poured into, one of the deck chairs that formed a ragged line two feet beyond the glittering water of the pool.

My watch said it was 6:57, but my stomach certainly was not ready for breakfast. A cup of hot coffee I could have used. Also, a hand in getting out of the sagging canvas seat. My legs weren't at full strength and lights rippled around the inside curve of my skull. My stomach churned, bile rose in the back of my throat, and my breath was sour in my nostrils. Maybe I hadn't thrown up all over myself, but it sure smelled like I had.

Disgusting to discover myself in such a state. I acknowledge that. Worse, it wasn't the first time. Clearly I'd allowed myself to disintegrate into a sorry specimen. In that crystalline sunshine it was outrageously clear. It was just as clear that I wasn't going to do anything about it, not this morning. For the moment it would be enough to get out of the chair.

It took me a couple of minutes, but finally I was erect, working on mobile. Moving like a tired fighter in the final round, I started for the patio door. Halfway there I changed my mind. I really didn't want to see Preston this morning. Next time I saw him I'd tell him what a great party it had been. Besides, I didn't look so hot right now and I could remember only fragments of the night before. A dark certainty that I had made a spectacle of myself gnawed at my brain.

I stumbled across the lawn and onto the sidewalk. The five miles ahead of me loomed like the Bataan Death March. Sweat was already forming across my brow and under my arms and my shirt was plastered to my back. Tugging off Jerry's tie, I stuffed it in an empty pocket. The tie was no longer unstained.

Just before Woodburn merged with Richmond Road I stumbled behind a forsythia bush and puked my guts out. After that I felt better and my walking developed a rhythm. My head still felt like someone had cracked it open with a dull axe and I still smelled like a Detroit dumpster in August, but I'd decided to live.

It was one hell of a long walk home and I had plenty of time to think. Most of the time it was how to put one foot in front of the other without falling down.

Then, just this side of the Glenn's Creek subdivision, it occurred to me that I should be able to get the redhead's telephone number from Preston. I vaguely recalled that she had been quite nice when she turned down my exquisite invitation to slow dance the night away.

Anyway, it was easier and safer to think about visions like that than my personal problems. Been that way for as long as I could remember. Change suddenly seemed to me to be a strange, perverse creature. It was continuous, automatically going on all around you, as natural and certain as the movements of the sun. Stopping change was not something a man could do. Yet, try to change one habit on your own, no matter how small, and you'd find out how excruciatingly, maddeningly difficult it was.

5

September ushered in a dry spell which stalled my lawn mowing service. For twenty bucks I helped a friend of a friend move, I made seventy-five dollars helping roof a house, and I made an even hundred, plus a bottle of Jack Daniels, helping unload a truck full of whiskey that had gotten lost on the way to Pittsburgh. That last job proved that there were advantages to hanging about in gin mills and low-life redneck bars.

I realized I was walking a tightrope stretched between skyscrapers, and that the tightrope was starting to sway in a rising breeze. I didn't plan to fall.

I spent several evenings lifting weights at Jerry's and ran whenever I was in the mood and the sun low enough on the horizon. I also took long walks and watched what I ate. Not that these final two behaviors spoke highly of my self-discipline. I didn't own a car and my pantry was nearly empty.

When I could I caged a beer, and bought one when I couldn't. Never did get around to calling Preston Marshall for the redhead's phone number.

I was on the verge of asking Pete, the midday bartender at The Final Furlong, if I could borrow the phone when a man I knew opened the door. His name was Fred Perry, and he'd given me jobs before. One had been a bit shady and the other strictly illegal, but I knew him from his days at the University of Kentucky, before he flunked out and moved on to making money.

Fred stepped inside and surveyed the place as if he were thinking of buying the building. He spotted me, hesitated, then went on down the line of drinkers at the bar like a sergeant reviewing his troops before he came back to me.

This time he made eye contact and gave me the sign. I gave him five minutes to get set up at a table in the back, then went to join him, carrying what was left of my beer in case he wasn't buying.

Fred looked me over like a butcher buying a steer before he jerked his long narrow head in the direction of an empty chair that had a cracked red leatherette bottom and featured a small, dark stain shaped like Cyprus.

"Fred."

"Kohler, how's it hanging?" Fred's voice was raspy. Too many Camel cigarettes and bottles of Old Granddad.

"Getting by."

"Making any money?"

"Nothing steady." I arched my eyebrows. "Could always use more."

Fred pulled a cigarette from the pack in his shirt pocket and put it between fleshy lips. He flicked his lighter and took a couple of drags, staring at me through the smoke without blinking.

He rubbed his jaw and cleared his throat. "Want a job?"

I took a sip of my beer. It was getting warm and going stale. It was also the only one I could afford that day. "Doing what?"

"Driving."

"Car or truck?"

Fred rubbed his forehead as if he had a headache, or was trying to stimulate his brain cells.

"Both."

"What do you mean?"

"Car down, truck back."

"Down where?"

"Mexico," Fred mumbled through the smoke.

"Mexico?"

"Yeah."

"Why?"

Fred took a look around the room. All I could see was a pair of tired waitresses and a smattering of bored losers. Fred must have been satisfied, because he leaned back in his chair and bared yellowed teeth.

"Man in Juarez wants the car. My boss wants what the man in Juarez has in his truck."

"Car hot?"

"It will be."

"Porsche?"

"Ferrari."

"It's in the VIP lot at the airport. Don't worry. Another man will be there. He knows what to do. All you are along for is to give him back-up and help drive." He fixed his eyes on mine. "Any more questions, Kohler?"

His tone irritated me. I swallowed the irritation. "When?"

"Saturday night. Leave at midnight. Owner is going to Chicago for three days. Theft won't hit the wires until he gets back. We're boosting it at the airport."

"All I do is drive?"

"Yeah, you and this other guy, switch out, sleep, keep moving."

"Who is the other guy?"

"Joe."

"Joe who?"

Fred mashed out his cigarette and glared at me. "Just Joe. That's all you need to know."

I nodded. "Okay, how much?"

"Two thousand. One now, one when you deliver what my boss wants."

"Deliver where?"

"Memphis."

"What's in the truck?"

Fred leaned across the table. He was close enough for me to smell the smoke on his breath. "You ask too goddamn many questions. Can't you get it through your thick skull that it would be better if you didn't know? Understand?"

"Yeah, Fred, I understand. Just one more question."

"Okay, what is it?" Fred scowled, tired of me already.

"How do I get home from Memphis?"

He snickered. It wasn't a pretty sound. "Your problem, buddy. Man with two thousand ought to be able to figure it out." He stood up and looked down at me. I could count the hairs in his long thin nose. "You want the job or not?"

"Give me the money."

Fred and I went to the john and he palmed me the cash. He left first. I sat back down at my table. My beer was still there. Like I said, the waitresses were tired. I picked up the mug and drained it.

6

Not a soul was stirring in the black asphalt night. A waning moon shone dully. Floodlights were few and widely spaced. Even under their faint glow it was easy to see why someone would want this car.

When the meager lights hit it just right the car sparkled like red crystal. Knife-sharp angles sliced the night until it bled heavy sticky darkness.

My partner was close to six-three, and he would go 240. Thirty pounds of that was in the gut that distended from his blue shirt like an overripe watermelon. I knew his name was Joe, that he smoked Camels, took cream with his coffee, and disliked small talk. Outside of that I didn't have a clue.

We were walking down Row H, dodging cracks in the pavement and shadows that flickered with the wind. Our prize was in slot 82. Except for a pickup exiting at the far end we were alone. No one had been behind us when we pulled our ticket out of the buzzing entry kiosk, or when we parked our Honda Civic. I wondered how long it would take the police to find it after the owner reported it stolen.

Joe walked with long, heavy steps, like a determined bear on his way to the berry patch. It was a warm night, but he wore a loose fitting blue jacket that hung down over his ample waist. My guess was he had a pistol stuck in the waistband of his sans-a-belt slacks, or in a shoulder harness.

"Got a key?" I asked.

Joe turned and gave me a look that indicated I was the stupidest shit he had ever been sentenced to work with. "No, I'm going to hot-wire the mother right here in front of God, the Holy Ghost, and the Virgin Mary. What are you thinking? Hell yes, I've got a key."

"Where did you get it?"

Joe kept on plodding across the black asphalt. "From his wife," he said out of the corner of his mouth.

"Why would she do that?" I felt like an innocent abroad, but figured I should know a few facts.

"She gets a cut of the profits." Joe gave me a look I interpreted as a leer. "Way I figure it, she's messing around and wants cash to spend on her boy-toy. Word is her old man has tons of money, only he's tight with it except when he wants something."

We were approaching the Ferrari. I wondered who was going to drive. Everything I'd done up to now had been minor league, just a toe across the line. Inside my skull the *Dragnet* theme was playing. I could hear Joe Friday's staccato voice, "It was a dark Saturday night in Lexington, Kentucky. Frank Kohler was working on grand theft auto, and a life behind bars."

Actually, life outside of them hadn't been so hot the past few years. College glory days were so far gone they seemed to belong to someone else. I tried to pinpoint where I had gone south. I gave up quickly; it didn't seem to matter anymore. Not to me, nor anyone else. Couldn't see where I had a whole lot to lose. Might even get permanently dried out while I was inside. That's how crazy my mind was working.

Joe stopped and jerked his head at the passenger door. "Get in. I'll take the first shift. You can get some sleep." He walked around to his side of the gleaming machine. I heard the key turn in the lock. I closed my eyes and took a deep breath. Then I opened the door and started sliding my backside across soft leather.

7

He drove like he walked, hard and fast, as though he saw himself personified in his car; bigger, swifter, stronger than the rest of humanity. He relied on the power of the Ferrari, and the weakness of the other drivers' nerves, to avoid head-on collisions. He hugged the white line in the middle of the road like it was his security blanket. The Ferrari had to work hard in the curves, tires squealing as it clung to the asphalt. If Joe was worried about getting pulled over for speeding he didn't show it. Instead, he stuck a dark brown cigar between his puffy lips, shut his face, and drove like his tail was on fire.

My silent partner and I crossed Kentucky in soft moonlight, going low and fast beneath the dying crescent. We stopped for gas and coffee in Bowling Green and switched drivers in Nashville.

The pent-up fury of the Ferrari felt strange beneath my palms. I'd never driven anything like it. The steering wheel throbbed like the pulse of a living creature. There was little traffic on I-40, and, following Joe's example, I put my foot down. Memphis loomed large on the horizon long before I expected it.

Blues dominated the radio waves and I found Howling Wolf and Muddy Waters, John Lee Hooker and Leadbelly. Their low, guttural moans filled the Ferrari with a harsh, lonely chant and turned the thermostat up on the atmosphere. In the flicker of lights from the roadside retreats I could catch backlit glimpses of Joe's face. He slept like a baby, a big ugly baby, with a five o'clock shadow along his jowls and a brutal mixture of tobacco, coffee, and Old Granddad on his breath. I blew through Tennessee like a fast moving cold front and set out across the Land of Opportunity.

Joe woke up with a jerk and a grunt just east of Little Rock. We changed drivers at a gas station off of I-30. I climbed into the passenger seat and settled back as he rocketed onto the interstate. My eyes were suddenly full of grit and I felt like I hadn't slept in a week. I closed them and tried to think of what I would do with my share of the payoff. I went to sleep worrying about how low I'd sunk.

Daylight was pouring in through the glass when I woke. I needed a drink in the worst way but Joe was wheeling into the gravel parking lot of a concrete block diner. A vulgar yellow sign promised the best ham and eggs in Texas. Joe filled the tank while I went in and secured a booth.

Morning was no kinder to him than the night before had been. He still looked ugly and mean and ready to tell the world to kiss his fat ass. I ran the palm of my hand along my left jaw line and listened to stubble rustle.

"What'll you have, boys?" The waitress was fat, with a mole on her chin, and she constantly shifted her weight from one foot to the other as if they both hurt. She reminded me of my Aunt Beulah, on my mother's side. Aunt Beulah drove Bus 47 for the Henry County School System and put up with Uncle John's whiskey drinking and womanizing.

I looked around for a menu, but this place was one of those where you didn't need one. Joe ordered steak and eggs and orange juice and coffee. I went with pancakes, two eggs over easy, and coffee. Aunt Beulah gave us a lukewarm smile, then wobbled off toward the kitchen.

The coffee was surprisingly good. I drank mine black. A prior occupant of our booth had left us a *Kansas City Star*, the two-day old version. Still, it was more entertaining than anything else in the restaurant.

The eggs were overcooked, but the pancakes were decent. Joe ate in silence, without ceasing, moving like some giant eating machine from steak to eggs, then back again. I gave up after one egg and half the stack. Beulah poured us another cup of hot coffee. I'd have rather had a nice cold beer.

I studied Joe through the rising steam. He was going through the half dozen pieces of paper he'd pulled from his shirt pocket. It was painful to watch his lips laboriously spell out each word. His thick fingers moved slowly across, then down the page.

Suddenly the morning was heavy on my shoulders. "Tell me something, Joe."

He raised his massive head slowly, as though it were difficult for him to tear himself away from his notes. A yellow dot of egg yolk punctuated one corner of his mouth. "What's that?" he grumbled.

"How did you ever get into this?"

"Into what?" He gave me a flinty-eyed stare that didn't help my digestion.

"Into this line of business."

"What business?"

I sensed I was on a dead-end road, but I persevered. "Trips like this."

He leaned over the table until I could smell his breakfast. "Shutup, dumbass."

"What?"

"Shut the fuck up about me and my business. Learn one thing, Joe College, and learn it fast. Keep your mouth shut. Understand?" He picked up his check and tossed a crumpled bill on the table. "Now let's go before you tell the whole world our business." He stood up, gave me a final glare of benediction, then walked toward the cash register without a look back.

I sat for another minute while my blood cooled. I was a long way from home, and rather at loose ends. I needed Joe to run inter-ference. At least that's what I told myself. Under my breath I said, "Fuck you and the horse you rode in on." Then I slid out of the booth and followed the man with the plan out the door. We didn't say another word until we crossed into Mexico.

8

We hit Juarez ahead of schedule, hungry, thirsty, and road-weary. Joe seemed to know where we were going, and that was a good thing. I'd forgotten ninety percent of the Spanish I'd learned as a sophomore at dear old Frankfort High. I recognized only an occasional word of the flashing neon.

Joe pulled the Ferrari into the parking lot behind a cantina off Hidalgo. We didn't have much company, just a couple of old Volkswagen Bugs, a late model Ford, and a dog with the mange. My partner told me to guard the car, switched off the motor and pocketed the key. He walked inside without looking back. I could see he was a very goal-oriented guy.

I watched the old dog scratch at his privates. Juarez was like the inside of a dirty oven. Sweat formed on my brow and ran down my cheeks until it pooled under my eyes. It plastered my shirt to my back and dampened the insides of my thighs.

There was nothing in the car to read except for a couple of gasoline receipts and the back of a pint milk carton that told about a missing twelve-year-old girl from Fort Worth. Joe had the key so I couldn't even listen to music. Not that it mattered much. Words would have been in Spanish.

In a few minutes he came out with two brown bottles of Mexican beer and a scowl on his face. He crossed the parking lot in half a dozen long hard steps and yanked the door open. The beer came in first and one came over my way.

"Thanks."

"Forget it, we got to go somewhere and hole up for a day."

I tilted the bottle and took a long drink. It was cool and wet. "Why the delay?"

Joe took a swig of his beer, then turned the key in the ignition. The motor roared to life and Joe wheeled the Ferrari out of the parking lot like a man with a purpose. All he said was, "The man just said we were to wait."

The Mexican night was black and the winds were hot and strong, rolling off desert sands with a peculiar vengeance. In five minutes we'd departed the main drag. Streetlights became fewer and farther between. Houses appeared small, nesting in tiny yards. Old cars that had given up the fight lay rusting amid garbage that lined the low curbs.

Traffic faded to a dull roar and my ears caught streams of sound that flowed from open cantina doors. In the suddenness of street-lights and the undulating pools of light pouring from unshuttered windows and open doors I saw a cacophony of mankind. Business-men in narrow-striped suits shut their doors against the night, bare-footed children, trailing laughter and final shouts of innocence, raced homeward toward supper and security, ladies of the night paraded precariously on pointed heels, making a sacrificial journey that promised only temporary respite from their darker side of the world.

I drank my beer, wanting another more with each taste, and wondered how close I was to their darkness. Hadn't always been that way; I used to have dreams. Where had they all gone? Life had a way of slipping away like water through your fingers. Maybe there were answers in Mexico, I told myself, knowing that the answers really comes only from inside. I was deluding myself, but self-delusion seemed easier than dealing with reality.

We twisted through a labyrinth that grew darker and more convoluted with each turn. Once, Joe slowed and pulled over to the curb where he spent a few seconds consulting his closely guarded notes. Then he shifted gears and we pulled away with a sharp bark from hot tires.

Night fed on itself until it became mammoth and we were merely a speck of dust floating just beyond the finger of eternity. I became so disoriented that I no longer even knew in which direction we were headed. My mind seemed to be drifting. I saw it as an asteroid floating through deep space and wondered if I was going insane. Then it occurred to me that perhaps I had been insane and was now trying to work my way back across the border. A man can have strange thoughts in a foreign land, especially when he's sober.

Without warning, Joe twisted the wheel violently and we were traversing an alley so narrow that each of us had only to extend an arm and we would be touching brown adobe walls that loomed above us like medieval fortifications. He drove as hard and fast down the long dark narrow corridor as he had on the wide boulevard. I was strangely unafraid, as though control of my life had been taken out of my hands. It wasn't an unpleasant sensation. Settling back against the soft leather of the Ferrari, I watched the world whirl by as we sped toward the fate that awaited us in the blackness that was Juarez.

9

Ebony hair flowed around her round brown face like a greasy river. Black eyes too large for her face glowed in the darkness with a startling luminescence. My fingers explored old pockmarks on her cheeks and ran across her dry cracked lips. They felt as wide as the flat side of my fingers. Under the thin, multi-colored blanket, we were both naked, and drunk on tequila.

Her name was Juanita and she lived somewhere in Juarez. "Nearby" was all she would tell me. She swore she was twenty-one, and her body backed her up. Her attitude toward sex with a drunk, dirty gringo was cavalier, tinged with a measure of greed. Yet something about her face gave off an aura of innocence. Perhaps it was those eyes. Life had been hammering at her, hard blows, but they hadn't knocked all the youthful vitality from those two great dark pools that threatened to devour her face.

Beneath the blanket her full breasts pressed softly against my chest. Her plump curve of belly spread out across my torso. Juanita's command of the English language was limited, but she could pronounce my name. She said it over and over, with the faintest of lisps, her mouth caressing my unshaven cheek.

Tilting the bottle up, I drained the last half inch of the liquid. Then I let it slip from my fingers. It struck the floor with a distant thud. I pulled the striped blanket up around us and kissed her on one corner of her mouth. Her breath was sweet and the taste of tequila was on her lips. The musky, ripe scent of her body filled my nostrils. I felt myself growing hard again, and I cupped her ample bottom in my hands and pulled her to me. She moaned softly as I entered, and I we rocked until sweat broke out and ran down my back and chest, moving as one in a rhythm more ancient and exotic than even Mexico herself.

She cried out, the sharp shrill cry of the thorn bird, and mashed her lips against mine. We bruised each other. I felt the eruption building. I said her name and felt her shudder as I exploded.

A curl of Mexican moon had risen against a backdrop of ebony. As we lay spent, I watched moonlight seep through the curtainless window until it bathed us in silver. We were merely two wandering souls who'd lost their way in a universe grown too vast. Her breasts rose and fell in rhythm to her faint, ladylike snores. She was sweet and beautiful in the moonlight; a lady of the night, mine to hold, if for only a heartbeat in eternity. So I held her close and kissed her shuttered eyelids and said her name as though it were a benediction.

10

The morning sun was hot and nasty. I lay with it full in my eyes and thought of thirty-seven ways to die. Each was unique and all seemed more appealing than trying to live with the deep fissure separating my skull in half. Survival seemed impossible. The only uncertainty seemed to be how long I would have to endure the pain.

In an effort to find relief I shifted my body downward along the couch and let my head roll off the upholstered armrest. Waves of nausea washed over me like high tide crossing a flat beach. I lay very still and waited for the waves to subside. I promised myself I would never drink again.

Based on past performance it was a promise I'd break before the sun in my eyes dropped beyond the western horizon. But I kept telling myself it was truth, willing myself to believe, willing myself to be the man I could be, not the one I was. Somewhere I'd read that it was never too late to become the man you were intended to be. In a morning that felt like a foretaste of hell, I permitted myself to believe that those words might be true.

When I woke again Juanita was gone, but my headache was not. Acting out of desperation, I forced myself up and went in search something to ease the pain. After a brief search I found an enamel medicine chest clinging to the peeling plaster wall above a dirty sink in a small bathroom. The plaster had faded to a pale green as if most of the color had evaporated. Glancing in the grime-smeared mirror that fronted the medicine chest I could see that same greenish tone coating my face.

I found three bottles of moisturizing lotion, a half-used stick of deodorant, one tin of Band-Aids three-quarters full, and two identical pink bottles of anti-diarrhea medicine. Some of the labels were in

Spanish and some were in English. A fine layer of dust covered them all. Just as I was beginning to despair, on the very back of the third shelf, behind a sky-blue woman's razor with a rusty blade, I located a bottle of aspirin.

I maneuvered the bottle around the razor and out of the medicine chest. Popping it open, I discovered three rather ancient aspirin. They were beginning to crumble to powder, but I raised the plastic bottle to my open lips and tilted it up. In the kitchen I found a half-full bottle of tequila and washed the taste out of my mouth. Always had heard not to drink the water in Mexico.

Two hours later Joe stumbled down the stairs and into the living room. His hair was uncombed and his face was still unshaven. One of his shoes was untied and his shirttail flapped below his waist like a spent sail. Yawning and scratching his ample backside, he ambled across the room. He looked bad enough at night; in the light of day he was downright disgusting. Closing my eyes, I tried to roll back over but the couch wasn't wide enough. I hoped he could take a hint.

Joe's footsteps were flat and loud. He didn't stop until he was close enough for me to smell the stale cigarette smoke, old sweat, and used sex that emanated from his skin and clothing. I kept quiet and listened as he rattled in his shirt pocket for his pack of cigarettes, then flicked his lighter. The smell of fresh smoke aroused a longing in me. The longing was for a drink.

"Get up, lazy ass. We've got a job to do today."

"I thought you said tonight," I mumbled into the back of the couch.

"Yeah, well, plans change."

I shrugged. I didn't have a lot of choice in the matter. "Give me an hour."

"You've got twenty minutes."

I kept my face buried into the fabric of the couch until the last echo of his footsteps died.

11

We turned from the blinding sun of Penasco Street into a narrow, dark alley. Buildings rose flat-faced above us, blocking the sun. Even craning my neck I couldn't see over the tops.

Painted walls rose only inches away from the speeding Ferrari. Joe drove like it was on rails. The alley was obviously a one-way street. I hoped we were going the right way.

"What's your hurry?" I shouted above the roar of the rushing wind.

Out of the corner of his mouth, Joe shouted back, "They're waiting."

"Where?"

"You'll find out."

I sat back and closed my eyes and let the wind mash against my face. Tires squealing, Joe wheeled the vehicle left onto a different street. This one was broader and came complete with curbs, gutters, and neat little bungalows set well back from the pavement.

In less than five minutes the complexion of the street began to change. Bungalows grew larger, farther apart, surrounded by better landscaping. Gradually, the road edged south and began a slow, laborious climb toward the crest of a mesa.

Cacti dotted hillsides like lonely sentinels. Dust hung in the air now and pockets of sand lined the road. Small dark birds crossed the road in front of us, flying low and hard.

The road dissolved into a series of switchbacks that Joe took at forty. We flattened out from the last one and looming before us was a massive iron gate, flanked on the right by a small concrete blockhouse, on the left by a pair of matched Dobermans. Joe braked the Ferrari to a stop five feet in front of the gate. We sat and listened to silence close in.

A short man with a long-barreled gun came out of the blockhouse. He wore khaki pants and a quasi-military shirt and hat. The gun barrel was oily black. It gleamed in the white-hot sun.

The short, dark man came around to Joe's side of the Ferrari. The rifle was pointed in our general direction. The man's right index finger was on the trigger. I wished for a weapon of my own, but I was starting to shake so badly I'd probably have shot myself. I needed a drink.

"Let me handle this," Joe mumbled without taking his eyes off the man with the rifle. I nodded like I thought he could hear me. My face felt flushed.

The dark little man stopped suddenly. His eyes swept down the sleek sides of the Ferrari, then came back to our faces. Too quickly for me to understand, he spoke a handful of words in Spanish.

Joe answered in Spanish. Then he turned to me. "Keep quiet and be cool. We just have to do this deal. Then we can head home."

"Okay." In the heavy silence I could hear teeth chattering against each other. They were mine. I hoped nobody else could hear.

The man with the rifle went back to the guardhouse and pushed a button. The big iron gate swung open and Joe eased the vehicle through the opening. The Dobermans never moved, except their eyes followed us all the way.

Blacktop cut across the green lawn in a wide ribbon. Sprinklers were on and water rose and fell across lush greenery. Miniature rainbows danced in the air above pink and white blossoms. The Ferrari growled along in low gear. We circled a massive flowerbed of yellow flowers and small statues of animals. From the center of the bed a silvery metal flagpole rose fifteen feet in the air. The tri-colored Mexican flag flapped in a stiffening breeze.

Three men in light-colored sport coats and slacks met us at the terminus of the drive. Their jackets were opened, and it was easy to catch the flash reflecting off metal.

The tallest of the trio walked casually around to the driver's side of the Ferrari. He spoke softly in well-modulated Spanish. Joe showed him his empty palms. Then, very slowly, he opened the glove compartment and pulled out a long white envelope. Two-thirds of the trio now had pistols in their hands. The sun was hot on my neck.

Joe gave the envelope to the unarmed man. He opened it and read it slowly and carefully. Twice. Then he put the letter back in the envelope and spoke to Joe. Stepping back from the car, he put the envelope in his coat pocket with one hand and took out a nasty little pistol from his shoulder harness with the other. Everybody in Mexico seemed to have a gun. Except me. My lack of firepower made my legs quiver.

Joe inclined his head my way. I tried to focus on his eyes. They told me nothing.

"I've got to go inside for a few moments to settle this deal. Wait here for me, and do it quietly. No stupid tricks."

"Don't worry, I'll be a good boy."

He nodded. "Ten minutes and if all goes well we pick up our load, then hit the road."

"Sounds like a winner to me."

Two of the men went with Joe. Watching Joe's broad back as he walked toward the front door of the hacienda, I wondered if I would ever see him again. Not that I was exactly fond of him, but without him I felt too much like the Lone Ranger. A rather defenseless one at that.

The old saw about any port in a storm kept drifting through my mind. As Joe stepped into dark shadows layered before an open door I could see that a thick streak of sweat ran the length of his back. In a strangely detached manner I found myself wondering if the sweat was a result of the heat, or fear.

Minutes multiplied upon themselves and the temperature rose until the Ferrari was an over-sized oven. When the sweat began to run into my eyes I got out and walked slowly around the pavement.

Under a flat roof that stretched above the cul-de-sac was a low stone wall that circled a fountain. The fountain was concrete, trimmed in bronze. It formed the shape of a Saguaro cactus. Water pulsed from each arm.

The man keeping an eye on me lounged against one of the pillars that supported the roof. A machine pistol dangled from his brown fingers. He sported a grease-pencil mustache and a cigarette dangled from his lips. Smoke curled upward until it dissolved above his thick curly hair. No lights flickered in his flat, mud brown eyes. I wondered if he had orders to kill me. For several reasons I wasn't just quite ready to die, especially not on a Mexican mesa top where the air was as clear as the crystal figurines my grandmother had collected.

I watched him smoke that cigarette, then light another. In the clean air, the acrid smell was vulgar.

What in the hell was keeping Joe? I needed a drink, very badly.

My sense of smell was strangely enhanced. In addition to the acrid smoke of my watcher's cigarette, I could smell the engine odor of the cooling Ferrari. Inside the house someone was cooking, and the scent of onions, peppers, and spices drifted to me on the stiffening breeze. I could smell the guard's aftershave and the unique odor generated by water from the fountain hitting warm sand and stone. The smell of my own sweat, and fear, was strong in my nostrils.

The thought that this might be my day to die tumbleweeded across my mind. I hoped it wasn't. I had no claim to greatness or glory, wasn't searching for a cure for cancer, or feeding the hungry, or writing the great American novel, yet I still was a life force, as much as any man. Standing there in the bright sunlight looking out across the flat brown earth that seemed to flow until it angled into the sky, I had a vision of my life as a unfinished painting, so many splashes of moveable color flung on a canvas by an unseen hand, still to be arranged. I had a visceral, cathartic urge to view the finished portrait.

12

Joe jerked his head at me as he emerged from the hacienda. For a moment he stood motionless in the bright sunlight, blinking sporadically like a gigantic, erect iguana. Then he began to walk down the driveway. I quick-stepped to catch up.

We matched strides across the asphalt. Sweat ran down my back. In my mind's eye there was a huge bull's eye painted on the back of my shirt. I listened for the burst of machine gun fire.

Joe fished out a cigarette from the pack in his pocket and stuck it between his lips. He didn't light it, whispering instead for me to "be cool."

There was no need for him to worry. I was ice, chilled to the bone. My hands shook so badly I put them in my pockets.

Twenty yards down the driveway asphalt spurs ran left and right. We took the one that bent left. It led to a five-car garage bigger than apartments I'd lived in. On the right side of the brick garage, backed in, was a faded yellow truck trimmed in brown rust. Joe pulled a key out of a pocket and opened the driver's door. I jogged around and climbed in the passenger side.

The motor sputtered on the first try, then died. The second time it coughed, caught, and rumbled to life. Joe eased out on the clutch and we began rolling in first.

We were in second, shifting into third, by the time we made the gate. It was still open and the little man with the long rifle was still leaning against the concrete guardhouse. He stared at us with unblinking eyes.

After putting ten miles behind us, Joe stopped twice in the next ten minutes. The first time was at a small grocery store. I sat in the truck with the motor running while he went inside. He came out with a loaf of bread, a couple of cans of pork and beans, one of Vienna sausage, a handful of candy bars, some chewing gum, a carton of Marlboro cigarettes with the health warning written in Spanish, and four brown bottles of Mexican beer. I was glad to see the beer. Didn't know if I would ever feel up to eating again.

The second stop took us a mile or so off the main highway. We wheeled to a halt in front of a low-slung adobe house with iron bars on the windows and a nervous Rottweiler out front.

Joe parked in the shade of a massive cottonwood that flourished along the roadside, and blew the horn--two longs and a short. An elderly man stepped out of a side door I hadn't seen.

The old man moved as if his joints were aching, but when he got close enough to see Joe's face his lips parted in a smile. The teeth he still had were stained and broken, but he said a half dozen words in Spanish with a voice that was strong.

Joe got out of the cab and shook hands. After exchanging what I presumed to be pleasantries, they ambled toward the ranch home without inviting me to join them. The Rottweiler raised his massive head but otherwise showed little interest. After the two men had passed he let his head flop back to the ground. His eyes were fixed on the truck. I sat on the warm, vinyl seat in the shade of the cottonwood and waited for Joe for the third time that day. I was getting good at waiting.

The breeze was not as strong here as it had been on the hillside and it grew steadily warmer in the cab, even in the shade with both windows rolled all the way down. My eyes felt full of desert sand. I wondered if I'd live to see Kentucky again. With an intensity that surprised me I hoped I would. I thought about the mess my life had become. Then I thought about football games I'd played in and women I'd known. Then all the images started going blurry.

The squeaking of the driver's door woke me. With one hand on the wheel, Joe pulled himself in. With the other, he stuffed a medium-sized brown paper sack under his seat. He fired up the engine and shouted "*hasta la vista*" at the old man as he swung the steering wheel. Half a mile down the road we were doing sixty and the truck was shaking until I thought it was going to shake itself apart before we hit the border. I started in on the beer.

13

Black and low to the ground, the Mercedes loomed larger by the second in the side-view mirror. We were twenty miles east of El Paso working our way through the foothills of the Hueco Mountains. Traffic was thinning with every mile and the road was finding blind spots in the dips and the rises.

Joe had the accelerator pushed to the floor. Above the roar of the wind I could hear the strain of the motor. Joe was flicking glances at the side mirror. Worry worked its way across his face like a rash.

I gave the passenger side mirror another look. The Mercedes was closing fast, showing no signs of slowing. Shifting my eyes back to Joe I asked, "Have they been there long?"

"Couple of minutes."

"They're closing too, aren't they?"

"Ramming speed."

The truck crested a rise steeper than the previous ones and started down. A sharp crack rang out. For an instant I thought it was the truck backfiring. Then Joe reached under the seat and dragged out the brown paper sack. He put it on the vinyl seat and pushed it across to me.

"Here, take this."

"What is it?"

"Look and see, numbnuts, and do it quick."

Another crack rang out and something pinged off the metal door at the back of the truck. I picked up the paper sack. It was heavy in my hands. Inside was a pistol. It was shiny black. A Colt. My hands trembled as I wrapped my fingers around the grip.

"Ever use one of those?"

"Just fooling around with a friend on his dad's farm."

"Well, you'd better get serious."

Another sharp report. Gunfire for sure.

My mouth was as dry as foot powder. All my saliva seemed to have migrated to the outside of my forehead. There it ran down my face as if an unseen hand had turned on a spigot. My legs trembled and I struggled not to urinate on myself.

"Move it, man. Goddamn it!" Joe jerked the wheel and we were two tires off the road, spewing gravel and raining dust. He twisted the wheel again and we swung back on the road moving in wide elliptical curves. Another shot rang out and I involuntarily ducked. I heard the bullet ping off metal, but the steering remained good. They must have missed everything vital. I figured they would go for a tire. Blow one and we were out of luck.

Joe was shouting but I couldn't understand him. I was afraid of dying and I wanted to scream. Instead, I cranked down the window and stuck my head out.

The angle was bad and the side of our truck occupied most of my field of vision. The only time I caught a glimpse of the Mercedes was when Joe zigged and they zagged. I squeezed the trigger anyway.

Asphalt and sagebrush were all I hit. The report of the pistol was a thunderclap in my ear. The wind whistling against my face was blinding, and tears rolled down my cheeks. I blinked them away as Joe maneuvered the truck through another slalom turn. The Mercedes slid into view. For an instant the flickering image of a dark face distorted by windshield glare reflecting the last remnants of the light of day flashed into my field of vision.

Firing left-handed, I squeezed off another shot. In response the driver of the Mercedes cut back to his left and they drifted out of sight. I heard a trio of pings as their return fire smashed into the rear of the truck.

More shots and Joe swore as the steering wheel spun in his hands and the truck veered sharply left. Muscles in his forearm bulged as he fought to keep the heavy vehicle under control. Sweat covered his face and in the dying daylight it had taken on an unhealthy sheen.

"Bastard got a tire. Can't hold them off long," he panted. "Better start doing some fancy shooting."

"Give me a target."

"What you see is what you get."

I think he was going to say something else, but before he could get it out there were more shots from the Mercedes. Glass smashed and metal pinged and the truck shuttered.

For a few seconds I thought Joe was going to be able to keep it on the road; then another tire went and we slid hard right, rolled across the uneven ground of the shoulder, crested the sand-covered hillock at the side of the road and were airborne. I braced myself and waited for the impact.

14

I woke up with a mouthful of blood and stars swirling before me. Joe moaned and I tried to move to help him, but my body was paralyzed.

Blinking my eyes, I shook my head and came to enough to realize that I was held fast by the seat belt. The truck had landed upside down, with my side of the cab a couple of feet higher than Joe's due to the slope of the land. I unfastened the belt and pulled myself up enough to slide out the window. The brown sand was still warm. The pistol was still in my left hand. Joe moaned again.

We were in a shallow arroyo covered in thick chaparral. I was on my belly looking through the low growth at an embankment. Beyond the embankment was the road.

It would take time to slow the heavy Mercedes and come back to the truck's launching point. However, I wasn't sure how long I'd been out.

Darkness was rapidly filling the arroyo, but the embankment was backlit by the setting sun. I scooted forward on my stomach into deeper brush, keeping my eyes on the crest of the embankment before me. Blood was dripping into my eyes like water leaking from a bad faucet. Switching the gun into my right hand, I wiped at the cut on my forehead with the palm of my left hand. It came back smeared with a warm, sticky, copper-colored substance that smelled of death. I turned my head slowly from left to right, then back again, trying to cover the forty to fifty yards of road's edge that was my field of vision.

Blood continued to drip into my left eye, so I shut it. The sky was growing darker and I felt weak and lightheaded. Pinpoints of light, dozens of them, danced before my eyes. The taste of my own blood mingled with the bile rising in my throat. I shivered. Maybe from shock, more likely from pure unadulterated fear.

I prayed that the men from the Mercedes would not wait. Cowardice weighted heavily on my mind. For a long time I hadn't been quite sure that living was worth the effort. Now, sprawled in the arroyo with the taste of my own blood in my mouth and men coming soon to kill me, I was sure.

The day had gone so quiet I could hear my own raspy breathing. Then Joe moaned. Then the quiet drifted back. Silence bore down on me like rocks and I moved my legs against the brush simply to break the spell.

At first I thought it was the call of a bird. Then it came again, off to my left, too shrill and discordant to be a bird. I turned my head just in time to see two dark shapes crest the rise. I twisted my body until I could see them coming carefully down the slope, their upper torsos still backlit by the dying rays of the sun. I swung the gun up, swallowed blood and bile, and squeezed the trigger.

The man on the far left screamed. The other man's arm swung up, and I saw the flash as he fired. The bullet sang shrilly by my head before I fired at the flash. I heard a loud grunt and then a crash as he fell into the chaparral. He rolled all the way to the bottom of the embankment. Then he was still.

His wounded partner had worked his way back up the slope. I could see him now, just at the crest, trying to run. His right leg dragged behind him and made him slow. The man ran toward the setting sun and his back was to me, big and dark, an easy target. I fired again and the man's arms flung away from his body as he pitched forward onto the pavement.

I'd been holding my breath and now I gasped for air as I turned to see about Joe. An animal loomed darkly before me in the gathering dark. Then it moved and I saw it was a man. A dark-faced man holding a gun with a long barrel. The hole at the end of the barrel looked large enough to swallow me.

"Drop the gun, hombre, before I kill you, and I can kill you very quick."

For a second I hesitated. A terrified voice kept screaming inside my skull, "Don't do it. Don't give up the gun; he will kill you anyway." Then I heard the click as the hammer slid back, and I knew it was all over. My gun was low and parallel to the ground. I could never raise it in time to pull off a killing shot. My only choice was to try and shoot him in the leg and pray.

"Don't be stupid, señor. Drop it."

I sighed and lifted my eyes and said, "Okay."

Suddenly the air held a whirling sound and something long and dark smashed against the man's head and the gun exploded above me. Then the man was moaning and falling down on me and I jerked my gun up and fired my last shot at point blank range into his gut.

His bloody insides were splattered all over my face. I could taste his blood and smell his fetid death. I pushed his heavy inertness off and crawled toward the truck. Joe was limping across the sand.

I pushed myself off the ground and onto one knee. Joe extended a hand and helped me up.

"I thought I was a dead man. What happened?"

"A BFR, that's what happened."

"A BFR. What in the hell is a BFR?"

"Big Fucking Rock, you dumb shit. I hit the bastard with a BFR in the head. Spoiled his aim enough so you could shoot him."

"Thanks."

"Don't mention it. You took care of the others."

I swiped at the blood that still trickled down my face. I felt weak and sick to my stomach. I wanted to sit down, but didn't dare. "Guess we'd better get moving."

Joe pulled on my arm. "Not just yet. There is something we have to get out of the truck. We can't take all the shit, but we can grab the prime stuff. Come on and help me."

We stumbled across the uneven ground like two drunken bums. I realized the gun was still in my right hand. It felt heavy and nasty and alive. I flung it as far as I could into the brush. Fireflies flickered on and off above the sagebrush. A late breeze whistled low in the chaparral.

15

"Just drop me at the corner. I can walk from there."

"You sure? Drive you right to your front door."

"Thanks, but it's been a long ride. I need to stretch my legs."

We had traded the Mercedes in for a two-year-old, green Ford Taurus at the Dallas-Fort Worth Airport, and the Taurus in Memphis for a beat-up blue Chevy Cavalier that had died just outside of Nashville. Joe had made a couple of calls, and we ended up finishing our trek in a Chrysler with a faulty air conditioner. Joe wheeled the Chrysler to the curb just where McKinley meets Mount Adams Road. That left me several streets to cross and the better part of a mile to go, but I didn't mind. No sense in letting these boys know exactly where I spent my private moments.

I opened the door, but before I could get out Joe dug a sweat-stained leather wallet out of his left hip pocket and fished out a pair of folded bills.

"Here's some cash to hold you over till I can deliver the shipment." He jerked his head toward Nike gym bags lying like dead animals in the trunk. I had a good idea what their contents were. Whatever was in there had almost gotten me killed, and three men had died along a lonely Texas highway trying to get it back. What made it worse was that I'd killed them. Just thinking about that afternoon made me want to puke my guts out. Never again would I be the same man I'd been before Mexico.

"Thanks. That'll work." I stuffed the bills in my shirt pocket and slipped out of the vehicle.

"Hey, how will I get the rest to you?" Joe leaned across the seat and stuck his head out the open passenger window. "You got a phone?"

"Nah, no phone. You can find me at Grant's."

"Downtown?"

"Yeah."

"Sure? What if I miss you?"

"I'll be there just about every evening."

Joe nodded, stared at me, and then his head disappeared. Seconds later he pulled away from the curb. I stood for a moment reflecting on the downward cycle of my world. Now the acceleration had intensified. Silently, I cursed myself, knowing I was the only one to blame, trying once again to pinpoint where I had gone sideways, letting my mind do its best to comprehend why I thought I couldn't stand working in an office, or selling overpriced things to people who didn't need them. Some thought was scratching at the back of my brain; I strained to see it, but it was like looking through smoked glass. Then it flickered and was gone and I was standing all alone, waiting for something. I just didn't know what.

A dark bird winged its way west. When he disappeared I took a deep breath and then the first step toward Culpepper Street and my empty bungalow.

16

Like a tomato left too long on the vine, summer had wrinkled and shriveled. My Mexican money had been delivered as promised by Joe, and duly spent. Joe never spelled out exactly how he got the money. I figured out all by myself what had been in those gym bags.

I kept busy, filling the hours helping Joe and his associates with some extra warm stereo equipment, mowing yards, watching black and white movies on my spasmodic television, and, as long as the money lasted, drinking beer and whiskey. For a few weeks I had lots of friends and time ceased to drag. Even paid off a few debts.

I slipped over to Commonwealth Stadium a couple of times a week to watch the Wildcats practice. The staff was positive, the pundits optimistic, and the fans enthusiastic. To me, the team looked a touch small and a step slow, especially in the defensive backfield. Plus, their kicking game sucked. In the *Herald-Leader*, players promised a bowl game. But I had quit believing in promises during an earlier life.

17

A few weeks after Mexico, Joe had introduced me to Tony, a short man with wild, busy eyes. I helped Tony make a pair of delivery runs, one to Cincinnati, the other to Chicago. Tony spoke just a little more English than I did Spanish, but we got along. He was good at using his hands for sign language and I recognized a gun when I saw it. On the way back from the Windy City he told me that Big Joe had said I was a good hombre to have around when things got rough, especially if there was gunplay involved. Thus reputations are born.

Tony didn't pay as well as Joe, but the work beat mowing lawns, and I'd always enjoyed drinking more as the days got shorter and the nights grew longer. I knew, in a hazy sort of way, that I was going the wrong way down a long dark tunnel. Yet I lacked the will, or imagination, to change. After killing three men, drinking too much seemed a rather mild vice, not to mention an enjoyable one.

I was sitting in Grant's watching an exhibition game on the tube when Les Johnson walked in. The Lions were going against the Packers. After his second knee operation, Les had been given a tryout with the Pack. It had been his final tryout.

His shoulders almost filled the doorway and his torso blocked virtually all the light that played on the asphalt behind him. I watched his massive head move as his eyes wandered around the sparsely populated room. When they lit on me a satisfied smile slid into place. Les stepped across the floor like a bear with bad knees. A stool was open beside me and he eased his bulk down on the cracked vinyl. He gave the bartender hand signals that encompassed me, then turned his eyes to the television.

"Good game?"

"All right, I guess. Haven't been following it closely."

"Who's up?"

"Packers, sixteen to seven."

"Third quarter?"

"Just started the fourth."

The bartender brought us a mug of beer apiece and Les gave him a ten and told him to keep it. Randy Parker was tending bar and he took his tip to the other end of the bar and started polishing wood with a white towel. Randy had been around.

We sipped beer and watched the Browns drive to the Packers twelve before fumbling the ball away.

Les shook his head. "Coleman always did have bad hands. Remember seeing him fumble twice against Penn State on New Year's Day."

"First round draft choice though."

"Yeah, he's got the speed and the moves. Plenty of power, too. Just can't hang onto the ball in crunch time."

"Lot of pressure on a running back, especially in a big game."

Les tilted his mug back and let almost half the contents slide down his throat. "That's right; you made a few good runs yourself."

I took a sip of my beer. I'd already downed three and that smooth, mellow aura was beginning. "Not really. Oh, I carried the ball a few times, but when the game was on the line the coach always called Press's number."

Les turned his face away from the television and pointed it at me.

"Speaking of Press, he's been trying to get ahold of you."

"What for?"

"Wants you to go out to supper with him next Saturday."

"Why?" I was genuinely puzzled. I hadn't seen the man in years and now he was inviting me over for the second time in less than six months.

Les leaned closer and whispered. He was close enough for me to smell his cologne. "You remember, Beth, his wife?"

I nodded.

"Well, seems she likes you, and Press likes to make her happy, when he can."

"What does Beth have to do with this?"

"Can you keep a secret?"

"Sure."

"Good. That'll make it easier."

All the evasiveness was making me exasperated. "Make what easier?"

"Like I said, they want you to go out to dinner with them 'cause when they go out Beth likes to drink and she doesn't like to drink alone in public and, of course, Press, he doesn't drink."

"So, instead of being the designated driver, I am the designated drinker."

Les chuckled. "Yeah, guess so. But Beth did take a fancy to you at the party, and she said you two always got along."

"What does that have to do with anything?"

"Frank, it's important to Press to keep Beth happy. Don't ask me why. He'll tell you himself. Just trust me. Keeping Beth smiling is important."

He leaned his big head close. His cologne had a lemony fragrance. "A lot of Press's associates, people who are very important to his plans, don't care that much for Beth, especially when she gets drunk. Which is whenever they go out. See?"

"I see. One drunk won't mind another, is that it?"

"Crudely stated, but more or less the play."

"Why take her out at all if her drinking bothers him?"

"Well, I wasn't supposed to tell, but maybe it'll help you understand. Press is going to run for Senator this next election cycle and he needs Beth for the family vote. He'll keep her behind the scenes as much as possible, but they have to be seen together now and then. We figured you wouldn't mind helping Press out. Plus, Press is at a stage of life when the old times start to haunt a man's mind. He wants to gather the flock together, renew old friendships, that sort of thing. You're with us, aren't you?"

"Sure, anything for my old roommate. Besides, who am I to turn down a free meal and free drinks? Where and when?"

"Coach House at eight. I'll even pick you up."

"Don't bother. I'll get there myself. Got a friend who will loan me his car." Despite his best efforts a grin was tugging at Les's mouth. I couldn't quite see why me going to supper with Press made Les so happy. That grin bothered me, made me want to drink. I finished my beer in three gulps, without ever figuring out why Press was suddenly so desirous of my company. I didn't completely buy the Beth story, but decided to go along for the ride. At least for now.

Les gave Freddy the two sign and he brought us refills. When he set the mugs down I noticed Les's first one was still half full.

We watched the rest of the game while I drank two more beers. All that beer lubricated my tongue. It felt thick in my mouth and flopped of its own accord. For an hour, I rambled on about football and Buddhism and Edward Hopper. Around midnight, Les said he had to go.

We shook hands and Les leaned close. "You'll remember to be there Saturday won't you, Frank? Don't want to disappoint Press and Beth."

"Sure. Coach House at eight. Coat and tie?"

"Right." He clapped me on the shoulder with a dumbbell disguised as his hand, then turned to go.

"Les?"

"Yeah?"

"Always wondered, you know?"

"Wondered what, Frank?"

"Whether I would fumble in the crunch zone in the big game. What do you think?"

He didn't answer me with words, and I couldn't decipher the message in his black eyes. Then he laughed and smacked me on the shoulder, turned, and did his arthritic grizzly bear imitation all the way to the door. I watched it swing shut behind him. Then I swiveled around and moved his mug over in front of me. Damn thing was three-fourths full and I hated to see good beer wasted. Shame I didn't feel that way about my life. Oh, guess I did care; just not enough to do anything about it.

18

Urges. Sometimes a man gets urges. Can't help it. Just gets them. That's the only way I can explain it.

I was headed home the morning before my big dinner. I'd spent the night before drinking beer and swapping lies with old man Hall. Used to date his daughter. She'd left us both for a dentist in Cleveland. Actually, I drank most of the beer and he told most of the lies. Full disclosure, I only drank until two in the morning. Then I passed out on his faded green loveseat.

Mist was rising, white and wet and wispy, curling like hickory smoke into the autumn air as I walked across the morning. The sun was a hazy orange disc, mashed lopsided against a bluebell eastern sky. Damp grass was the color of ripe peas. Morning air was cool and crisp enough to eat. It cleared my head like a tonic. I felt dangerously good.

At the corner of Logan and Holly there is a small park. Not quite as long as a football field and perhaps two-thirds as wide. Benches were strewn haphazardly along the road frontage, accompanied by a concrete birdbath, one newspaper machine in the triangle where the two roads intersect, and a soccer goal rusting away in the far corner.

I think one of the YMCA teams uses it for practice when Jacobson Park is full. The rest of the space is simply flat green grass. You can run on it, throw a Frisbee above it, pass baseball with a buddy within its confines, or, as about two dozen young men were doing that early fall morning, play a game of sandlot football atop it. No pads, no helmets, no jerseys with names, no numbers or sponsors' logos. Just down three steps and out, cut right at the big mud hole, and fly toward the birdbath. The ball will be hanging out there for you to pluck from the mist. I wandered across the yielding turf until I was within twenty yards of the two huddles.

Didn't take me long to observe that the game was a rough and tumble version of two-hand touch that often degenerated into a thinly disguised tackling-without-pads approach that was far from gentlemanly.

A fat boy with red hair went down with a bad knee, and a skinny black man with a pencil mustache caught an elbow to the nose and left the field streaming blood. Both sides were developing a certain lean and decimated look.

The quarterback of the team that was behind yelled at me and a kid wearing a Paul Laurence Dunbar High jacket to join the game. If the jacket was his, the boy had lettered in track, basketball, and football. We jogged out together. I was shivering. Whether that was from the cool air or a rising excitement I wasn't sure.

The guy who'd called us out chose the Dunbar kid. I went over to a team headed by a man with a big mouth. He was five-seven at most, and might have weighed one forty soaking wet. We had the ball.

For the first half-dozen plays I was Knute Rockne reincarnated. I outran a guy in a Steelers jersey and a girl wearing braces on a post route. I threw a body block on a fat man with long hair on one play, then got off a twenty yard run. We scored when I out-jumped the Dunbar kid for a wobbly spiral in the left corner of the makeshift end zone. The ground rose up and smacked the breath out of me. Never really got it back.

Huffing and puffing, I played as hard as I could on defense. The first time they threw the ball my way, I batted it down. The second time, I tagged the man who caught it. The third time I had to cut sharply on grass still damp from the morning dew and I felt something tear in my left calf.

Playing hurt may be the name of the game at nineteen, but approaching forty it is no longer a viable reality. I hung in for one more series, then gave up my spot to a bald-headed man who looked like a backup librarian. Taking my wounded pride along, I limped on home to Culpepper. Four aspirins and three beers later life looked a little less like the end of the trail. Dreams die hard for foolish fullbacks.

Dreams like those were only memories to me, dreams whose names I did not know. Old sepia-tinted photographs hanging haphazardly on the walls of my mind, edges curling, fading to nihility.

19

That afternoon I helped a drinking buddy panel his basement. When I got home I drank a beer and a whiskey chaser and took a nap. After I woke up I had another beer before I showered, and laid out my clothes. While I was getting my head straight I watched John Wayne in black and white. Most film stars look better in black and white. A lot of the time so does life. Technicolor creates unrealistic expectations. I didn't need any more of those. Been having them all my life.

My best white shirt was clean. There was only a very small stain on my new tie, and my sports coat would cover that when buttoned. The label in the coat read Graves-Cox, and that store had been out of business for years. Couldn't even remember buying it. I brushed dust off the shoulders and slipped it on.

It was tight through the chest when I buttoned it and the sleeves seemed a touch short. The lapels were too wide and the hue hadn't been hot for ten years. I felt old and out of step. I began to regret agreeing to this supper.

George Disney lived over on Highlands Drive. He and I had shared a table at the Furlong a couple of times. George was all right, especially for a Republican who still loved Nixon. Retired from Lexmark, George drove for Bluegrass Cab Company to make beer money. Saturday was his day off and I made a small donation to his favorite charity and borrowed his cab. On the east side of the Coach House parking lot I found a spot in the deep shadows between a Buick Regal that was missing the left front quarter panel and a GMC pickup whose bed was rusted through. Vehicles that belonged to the kitchen help, I guessed. I didn't mind and didn't figure they would.

Since the last battery died in my Timex I haven't been the most punctual guy in the world. Still, I was only fifteen minutes late. As I followed Anthony, the maître d', I wondered if being fashionably late was still in vogue.

Four people sat at the table, Preston, Beth, Les, and a thin-faced, white-haired gentleman whose picture I'd seen in the paper.

Preston rose, a smile on his face. In a sharply-tailored navy blue suit that featured a razor thin pinstripe in a lighter shade of blue and fit him like a second skin, he looked younger than I knew he was. He stuck out his right hand. It was impossible to miss the horseshoe ring on his third finger. Enough diamonds encrusted the ring to make it look like a miniature mine.

"Sorry I'm late."

"No problem, we just gave Paul our drink order." Preston inclined his head toward a uniformed man bearing down on us with a tray sporting five glasses. "I took the liberty of ordering for you. Jefferson Reserve okay?"

"Sure." Like it mattered to me. Good buddy Press Marshall was paying. I was just along for the ride; might as well enjoy quality stuff.

"Frank, I'd like you to meet someone. This is T.R. Slone. Mr. Slone owns Pinecrest Farm. Mr. Slone, this is my friend and old Wildcat teammate, Frank Kohler."

"Pleased to meet you, Mr. Slone."

Now I placed him. In addition to maintaining one of the finest horse farms in Bourbon County, just south of Paris, he ran a major construction company, owned several key office buildings in Lexington, a significant piece of the third largest bank in the state, and a myriad of smaller companies. Worth millions, and making more all the time. Rumor had it he'd hand-picked the last two governors and our newly-elected mayor. His handshake was firm, but I could feel bones working beneath the skin. His blue eyes were clear and cold as Canadian air in late November.

"Likewise, and what do you do, Mr. Kohler?"

"I'm a consultant."

"I see."

"Frank, you know the rest of the gang. Sit down, gentlemen, and let's have a drink."

I sat down and sipped at my whiskey. I'd almost forgotten just how good fine whiskey tastes. Slone's drink looked like champagne.

Difficult to decide for sure what the other three were drinking, but Beth's was a double.

Service was first class and the food beautifully presented. The conversation flowed primarily between Preston and Slone, and focused on business or politics, or the business of politics, all of which I found boring. Again, I wondered why I was there. Oh, I'd heard the tale told by Les, but I wasn't buying it, at least not all of it.

Speaking of Les, he ate little and drank less. Mostly he leaned his ample bulk back in his chair and observed.

Beth mostly drank. She nibbled at a salad and ate a few bites of undercooked green beans, but didn't touch her chicken or boiled new potatoes.

She could drink; I had to give her that. She drank even more than I did, which is saying something, because I wasn't feeling any pain by then.

Halfway through my second glass of Jefferson Reserve, I felt a light touch at my elbow. I turned to find T.R. Slone's glistening blue eyes focused on me.

"Sorry."

He smiled. "I was just asking if you were interested in politics, Mr. Kohler."

"I vote."

"Naturally, but do you involve yourself with the intricacies of politics. I find them fascinating."

"Not anymore. I gave up on them during the Clinton deal."

"Oh, really. Why, if you don't mind my asking?" He showed me a mouthful of teeth. I wasn't sure whether he was serious or poking fun at me.

Buying thinking time, I took another sip of whiskey. "Guess I just got real tired of hearing about other people's private lives. Not to mention some degenerate old fossils trying to tell the rest of the world how to behave."

The old man leaned closer, establishing a sector of intimacy around us. "But wouldn't you agree, Mr. Kohler, that our duly elected officials have certain responsibilities that arise as a function of their office."

"Seems to me, Mr. Slone, that they have a responsibility to the people who elected them."

"A responsibility to lead them on a morally righteous path?"

"More like a responsibility to represent the electorate and their wishes, not to force feed the public the politician's own idiosyn-crasies."

"But our elected officials have much greater access to the facts, to the numbers that, in reality, run our lives."

"I don't need someone, or some Neanderthal organization, to tell me how to run my own life."

Slone chuckled. "Ah, a rugged individualist. Among the last of a dying breed." He looked as if he had more to say, but just then Paul came up and asked us with a lisp if we were ready for dessert. I ordered another drink and excused myself.

The night was rapidly going south. I couldn't see where this dinner had been any sort of a great success, or even why I had been invited. There was a sourness in my stomach and the smell of stale cigarette smoke permeated my nostrils. Excusing myself, I visited the men's room. As I washed my hands I stared at the face in the mirror. It took me a while to come up with an appropriate definition. Finally the connections inside my hard-wired mind clicked. Dilapidated.

I took the long way back to the table, curling through the parking lot, wandering under yellowish circles of the street lamps, sucking fresh air. A certain small voice inside me told me to get in George's cab and drive home without saying my good-byes. Not sure if it was the good whiskey, or simply stubborn pride, but I never got any further than putting one hand on the door handle.

When I got back to the table it was clear that the gang of four had been playing musical chairs. Preston and Slone had paired up at one end of the table, while Beth sat next to an empty chair at the other.

Les was running interference halfway between the empty chair and my old backfield mate.

A full glass sat in front of the empty chair. I sat down and stared at the dark liquid. My stomach was already gently churning. More Jefferson Reserve wouldn't calm the roiling.

"Come on, bottoms up, you old fullback," Beth mumbled. Her words were slurred and a cloudy look was rising in her eyes.

Picking up the glass, I lifted it to my mouth and let the liquid lap against my lips and then put it back down.

"Oh, come on. Drink up. You don't want to be a party-pooper." She pawed at the air ineffectually with her left hand.

I opted for diplomacy. "I've been doing my share. Seems to me as if your husband has been the one drinking light tonight."

Beth snorted derisively. "Oh, that's just Press. Always Mister Goody-Two Shoes, especially around big money. Afraid the All-American is not much fun anymore."

"What are he and Slone talking about?"

"Money, business, stocks and bonds, financial fusters, er, I mean futures. Some future anyway. Probably Press's. That's what interests him. In fact, that's the only thing he's interested in."

"Is he thinking about going into business?"

"My dear Frank, the one and only Preston Marshall is always thinking about business. He worships the almighty dollar these days, not the athletic ideal, nor his goddess of a wife."

Beth laid one soft hand on my arm, blinking like an owl in the glare of a flashlight. Her eyes had a familiar glazed look. I wondered how mine looked. Maybe not quite as glazed. The walk had helped clear out the fog and for some reason whiskey wasn't overly appealing tonight. Maybe I was reacting against Beth's overindulgence. I'd noticed that response before; I seemed to react more strongly against than for.

"Do you know, old friend, that my handsome halfback of a husband once worshipped me. At least he said he did. I used to believe him. Now I wonder. Since Daddy's money dried up I seem to have to turn to drink for companionship. Your old teammate is too full of ideas concerning himself these days to pay any attention to his wife."

I began to wish the evening were over, or that I had never come. Preston had tuned me out. Beth had turned into a drunken, bitter bitch. My head hurt and waves of nausea were slashing against my ribs.

Something tugged at the sleeve of my jacket. It felt like a small animal grubbing for food. The small animal turned out to be Beth.

"Frank."

"Yes."

"Frank."

"What?" I hoped she was too drunk to notice the irritation in my voice. She smiled and the whiskey on her breath mixed with the jasmine scent of her perfume. A particularly nasty combination.

"Do you think I'm attractive?"

"What? Yeah, sure."

"I used to be." Her hand worked at the fabric of my coat as if she were scratching fleas.

"I used to be beautiful."

My brain felt thick, whiskey and disgust and embarrassment all swirling together, and I couldn't think of a satisfactory comment. After a moment I nodded.

"I used to be so beautiful. Even Press thought so. He told me every night before we made love."

My voice was frozen shut. I glanced at Press. He was deep in conversation. I nodded again. The motion increased my nausea. I wondered why my stomach was acting up. In my time I'd drunk a good deal more with less effect. Maybe I was coming down with something.

"I used to be gorgeous. Now I'm fat. Fat and drunk and we never make love. Frank, did you know Preston doesn't even sleep in the same bed with me anymore?"

"No." But I could understand why.

"Frank?" Her eyes were focusing on nothing in this world.

"What?"

"Frank?" Tears gathered in the corners of her eyes.

"For god's sake, what?"

"Don't you yell at me, too," Beth sobbed softly.

"I'm sorry."

She sniffed and her eyes took on that faraway look again. Then she blinked and lifted her face. Her cheeks looked damp. "Frank, you want to know something?"

"Yeah, go ahead," I said. My brain felt like sludge. I couldn't seem to think clearly at all. Whiskey had never affected me like this before. The room was tilting ever so slightly. I focused my eyes on Slone's white hair, willing the tilting to level out.

Beth leaned close. Her hair caressed my face. She put her mouth against my right ear and whispered, "I used to be beautiful. I used to be a cheerleader and every boy wanted me. Now I'm old and fat and no man will touch me." The tip of her tongue caressed my ear. "Do you want me, Frank? Do you?"

I didn't know what to say. The room spun slowly and the evening rose up and gut-punched me. Pushing myself up, I stumbled toward the door. My chair clattered to the floor behind me and Beth screeched something unintelligible.

I barely made it out the front door before I threw up. I puked Jefferson Reserve and Louisiana quail and wild rice all over one of the little stone jockeys, the right rear quarter panel of a Mercedes 300S, and the shoes of the doorman.

19

There are times so bad that I just crawl up over the top of my own little world and slide down inside myself, closing the hatch tightly behind me. This was one of those times.

Somehow, I managed to pull myself together enough to stumble across the asphalt, find the key, stuff it in the ignition, and steer myself toward home.

Actually the steering wasn't hard, it was the navigation that presented difficulties. Cars, vans, and pickup trucks swam all around me in the murky streetlight glow. Suspended just below the surface of the night, traffic signals flashed, a concerto of red, yellow, green. Blurred and twisted and moving, normally inert street signs were illegible. Sounds from the cab radio were muffled. Streets that should have been as familiar as the back of my hand were strange and frightening. The night was like a bad trip I'd taken right after college when I'd smoked tainted pot.

In the tortured workings of my brain, I was a lost soul in a world spun out of control, doomed to travel forever on a quivering ribbon of blacktop that twisted back in on itself until it was little more than tangled asphalt fishing line wound around a dark labyrinth of withered trees and unsmoothable bricks. Pinpoints of golden light fluttered before my eyes like a thousand miniature fireflies.

Each passing minute seemed to add to the burden pressing on my shoulders. I wanted to scream, but what good would that have done. I had all but despaired of reaching home when my house suddenly loomed white and amorphous before me. Instincts and muscle memory have saved many a man.

Braking hard, I jerked the cab to a stop and cut the motor. Without warning, I was so sleepy that I didn't think I'd be able to keep my eyes open. My hands seemed far away and my fingers were slow to respond to commands. Everything went black and I felt my body swing out into the night and come back. I patted my checks and told my legs to move.

Don't remember unlocking the door or crossing the living room, but I blinked and shivered and fell across the bed. Not sure, or caring, if I was clothed or naked, dead or alive, in this world or the next, I pulled a blanket over my head, closed my eyes, and drifted into the beckoning darkness.

20

I woke up screaming, fear wrapped around my insides, a slimy umbilical cord. My heart was pounding as if I'd just sprinted the length of a football field. My clothes were soaked with sweat and I could smell a dark scent and taste bitter on my tongue. I wanted to cry. This time, I really needed a drink.

I flicked on the horse-head lamp that stood on the rickety bamboo nightstand next to my bed. The clock said four forty-five. A piss-poor time to die of fright.

Leaving the lamp on, I got out of bed and stumbled into the kitchen, flying on instruments. Stray pinpoints of light kept flashing on and off before me. The floor undulated gently beneath my bare feet and the walls swirled in a slow elliptical orbit. My muscles responded sluggishly, the way they used to when I got my bell rung on the football field.

Even in my own house I was strangely disoriented. Half the syapses in my brain seemed to be short-circuiting. I'd been drunk before, plenty of times, but never like this. I wondered vaguely, in that slice of my brain that was still functioning, if I had alcohol poisoning.

Swinging open the cabinet door next to the refrigerator I rummaged around until I found a new box of Rolaids and half full bottle of Bayer aspirin. I chewed and swallowed half a dozen Rolaids, then choked down four Bayer's.

I sat down heavily on one of the wooden kitchen chairs I'd borrowed from my mother's cousin in Richmond. Seconds later, I put my head down on the table and shut my eyes so I wouldn't see the room spin anymore.

Half of me wanted to die. The other half was afraid I would. My stomach turned over and before I could get to my feet I was puking my guts out.

I slid out of the chair and down on my hands and knees, still regurgitating whatever was left in my stomach. When it was all gone the dry heaves took over. When they had passed, I let myself slide the rest of the way down until my face lay pressed against cool linoleum.

The smell of my own vomit raged in my nostrils and in that instant I truly despised myself. It wasn't that I didn't want to move away from the stench. I simply could not. I just lay there on the filthy kitchen floor and let the darkness wash over me. Nothing about the evening had been quite right, and I surrendered gratefully to the nothingness.

21

A maniac was pounding away with a jackhammer. I could feel reverberations inside my skull. Now and then he would pause for a few seconds, only to start up again. My brain felt as though it might crack any minute.

I heard my name being called. The syllables were loud, but distorted as if they were trying to tunnel through solid matter. I tried to open my eyes to see what was happening. My eyelids seemed glued together. I tried again.

All I could see was linoleum and congealing vomit. My stomach rolled and I choked back hot bile. I pushed myself up onto my hands and knees. My arms and legs trembled beneath my body, but at least I had my face out of my own vomit.

My head spun, but two feet above the floor the air was better and I began to drift back into the real world. Someone was pounding on the back door and calling my name. So much for the jackhammer hypothesis.

"Hold on," I croaked, and began to work my way to erect. Eventually I made it, then staggered to the kitchen door. Using the door frame for support, I turned the handle and swung the door open. Fresh air hit me like a shattered ammonia capsule.

A man in a police uniform was standing outside my door. He looked at me with great interest from under the bill of his cap. He had bright blue eyes, hard and cold as marbles, a knife slit for a mouth, and a small wine-colored birthmark on his left cheek.

"Hello." My voice rasped like green wood being drawn through a saw.

"Mr. Frank Kohler?"

I wiped the back of my hand across my mouth. Scum adhered to my flesh. "Yes."

"Sergeant Reid, Lexington-Fayette Police. May I come in, sir?"

"Yeah, sure." I stepped back.

The sergeant wore a smile that didn't quite make it to his eyes. Tiny, round, blue, motorized cameras, constantly on the move, they were recording everything. I could almost see his brain compartmentalize and log each item. After he'd swept the room with his camera eyes he turned them on me. "Appreciate your cooperation, Mr. Kohler. May I ask you a few questions?"

"Okay." I wondered which of my recent activities had attracted the attention of Lexington's finest.

Reid slid a small spiral notebook out of his breast pocket and flipped the cover back. Then he pulled a ballpoint pen from the same pocket.

"Hate to be so forward with you, and it's probably a big waste of time for both of us, but I'd better read your rights to you."

He recited and I acknowledged. Reid tapped a front tooth with the top of his pen. "That your cab outside?"

"No. Borrowed it yesterday from a friend of mine."

"You own a car, Mr. Kohler?"

"No, I walk where I need to go, or catch a ride."

"Special occasion last night?"

"Dinner with friends." I couldn't see where he was headed with this line of questioning and that worried me.

"Where did you eat?"

"Coach House."

"Nice place."

"Very."

The sergeant tilted his cap back and scratched gently at the base of his hairline. "Course it's a little rich for my blood." He glared around the dirty kitchen with drying vomit still on the floor as if to imply it was also too rich for me. He was correct.

"I wasn't paying."

"That's nice. Mind telling me who was?"

I gave him the complete guest list. He jotted the names down in his little blue notebook without commentary.

After I'd finished he wandered around the room, looking closely at several items, including the garbage can and the kitchen sink. Then he turned back and looked me up and down. His face was devoid of expression. "What time was dinner over?"

"I'm not sure. I left early."

"How come?"

"I felt sick at my stomach." My eyes drifted toward the floor.

"Remember what time that was?"

I shook my head from side to side, slowly. "Sorry, no."

"That's okay. Your friends can probably tell me."

"I doubt it. Didn't exactly say good-bye."

"Did you quarrel?"

"No, just needed to get some air."

"So you simply left, without letting your host know?" He raised dark eyebrows at me.

"That's right."

"Why?"

"No particular reason."

Reid shrugged and wrote in his notebook. "Go straight home?"

"Yes."

"What time did you get home?"

It was my turn to shrug. "Didn't check the clock."

"Any particular reason why not?"

"No, Sergeant. I just didn't look."

His harping on the time was getting on my nerves. I wondered if it was supposed to. It occurred to me that this might be a time when the less I said the better. I hadn't done anything wrong, at least not that I could remember, but Sergeant Reid hadn't come to collect for the Policemen's Ball.

"Stop off anywhere along the way after you left the Coach House?"

"No."

"Sure?"

"Positive."

"Go anywhere after you got home?"

"No."

He looked up at the ceiling and rotated his head as if his neck muscles were stiff. Tendons worked beneath the skin. "Mr. Kohler, what would you say if we had a report of your cab outside the Red Dot Liquor on Nicholasville Road just before twelve?"

"I would say whoever reported that was mistaken."

"What if we had two reports of your cab leaving the liquor store at high speed just after it was robbed?"

"I'd say they were lying."

"Why would they do that?" He gave me a puzzled look.

Sweat was popping out all over, but I was chilled inside. I tried to remember the night before. I drew a blank. "Maybe the people who told you that they saw the cab really did the hold-up themselves."

The sergeant gave me a sad look as if I were a prize pupil who had just missed an easy question. "Maybe you'd better go to the station with me and Officer York."

A man I hadn't noticed stepped into the kitchen from the living room. I'd never heard the front door rattle. Probably hadn't remembered to lock it. Handcuffs clicked cold and heavy on my wrists.

22

The Lexington-Fayette Urban-County Detention Center was like most jails, acres of concrete and steel, surveillance cameras and bored guards and inmates, blended together with measures of self-pity and despair.

Erring on the side of caution, they read me my rights again at the jail, then let me make my phone call. Not being intimately acquainted with any lawyers, I called Press. He could confirm my attendance at the Coach House, vouch for my good character, and maybe say magic words that would spring me from the holding cell I was sharing with an extraordinarily tall black man, dressed in a brown suit featuring a wide, white pin-stripe, who smelled strongly of cheap wine. At least that was the way I had it figured. Then again, I had the hangover from hell and felt like I could cry any minute.

It took him an exceedingly long two hours to get down to the jail. Most of the time I spent telling the black man how it was all simply a big mix-up and that everything would be straightened out soon.

My cellmate slept straight through my soliloquy, snoring softly and politely. He didn't really hurt my feelings though. Way I figured it, he didn't miss much; I couldn't even make myself believe half of what I was saying.

Finally, a puffy-faced guard, with thick black hair that wasn't his own and a pot gut that was, came and led me to a room of small cubicles, where prisoners on one side of bulletproof glass could talk to their visitors on the other. I counted four cameras and seven guards. Figured they were taping everything. I could see Preston and he could see me, but we had to talk to each other via a sound system of ancient lineage and dubious quality. All of his words came to me slightly muffled, as though he was speaking through a layer of cotton.

Press started with small talk, but I cut it short. "Hold the chit-chat. When can you get me out?"

"Don't know, Frank. Seems the case against you is strong."

"What do you mean, strong? How can it be strong? I'm innocent, you know."

Preston just stared at me. A knot rose in my throat. I swallowed it.

"How strong?"

"Two eyewitnesses have given a fair description of you, and a better one of your car."

The pounding in my head began intensifying. "How good?"

"The license plate number."

"How close to the number?"

"Exact."

"Shit." The cubicle seemed to be floating and I was starting to sweat, which was strange because inside I felt as cold as ice.

"What in the hell did you use a damn cab for, Frank?"

"Use a cab for what?"

Preston shrugged and rolled his eyes. "You know, the liquor store deal."

"I didn't even go to the damn liquor store."

Preston gave me a long hard look; I felt like a goldfish on the other side of the glass. The back of my neck felt hot. "You sure?"

"Positive." Surely I couldn't have blacked out that long. Robbing anyone had never crossed my mind. Something wasn't right. Make that nothing was right. The whole night was lousy with unanswerable questions. I had a strange feeling that the universe was playing a grand joke on me.

"Then how can they have eyewitnesses?"

"How the hell should I know? Maybe the cops are making it up about the witnesses."

"I've got my attorney working on it. McChesney says no, the witnesses are legit."

"Maybe they enjoy lying." My mouth was dry and my words echoed in my ears. I licked my lips. They felt like sandpaper. "Or maybe they are covering for themselves."

"Not a chance. One of them was virtually in hysterics. She is the wife of the owner, the one who got shot."

Cold sweat dotted my forehead. I wanted to scream.

"Somebody got shot? Nobody said anything to me about that." My face felt flushed and my bowels were dangerous loose.

"Sorry, Frank. Looks like I spoiled the surprise."

"Ain't that a damn shame. How badly hurt is this guy who got shot?"

"Pretty bad. He's at Central Baptist. Caught the latest news on WVLK on the way down. Apparently it's touch and go."

"Damn."

Preston nodded. Funny what you notice at the critical times in your life, but I happened to observe that his hair didn't move at all when he bobbled his head up and down. "Reporter said the next twenty-four hours is critical."

"Yeah," I said, "for him and for me."

23

Black lettering on frosted glass read CAPTAIN LETHRIDGE. I stood between two uniformed officers, Perkins and Dunn. They moved about their appointed rounds with a grim determination. All the way from my cell in the basement they had studiously avoided letting even the edges of their uniforms brush against me.

Perkins knocked twice. He had faded blue eyes, freckles, and wore a silver wedding band. Something in his mannerisms reminded me of my cousin, Tim Lester. Tim used to shoot cats with a BB gun for kicks.

"Enter."

Perkins twisted the knob, pushed the door open and stepped inside. I followed with Dunn close behind. His breath felt hot against the back of my neck.

Lethridge's face was a hollowed out skull beneath a 1957 crew cut. He inclined his narrow head toward a straight back metal chair centered in front of his surprisingly modern-styled desk. I sat. The grim-faced boys in black stood.

"I remember you."

"What do you mean?"

"From when you played ball for UK." He stopped and rubbed the palm of his left hand across a jaw shaved so close it looked as smooth as glass.

"Always liked you back then. Maybe you weren't the star, but you were a real team player, hustled your ass off. Did whatever it took: blocking, running, catching the ball in traffic. In those days if it needed doing, you did it. Tell me, Kohler, what happened?"

I shrugged. "Nothing happened, Captain. I graduated, grew up. Life goes on."

"Looks as if it has been going downhill for you." He gave me a sad smile that he didn't really mean.

"I didn't do this liquor store fuck-up."

"Eyewitnesses say you did."

"Guess I ought to know."

He leaned forward and stared at me with a palpable intensity. "Are you sure? Hear you were so drunk that you could barely walk."

"I had a few drinks. That doesn't mean I robbed a liquor store or shot anybody."

"How would you know? We heard you were absolutely plastered. Disappeared in the middle of a dinner party."

Nasty icicles of fear were forming at the base of my skull. I asked, "Who have you talked with?"

Lethridge leaned back in his chair and folded his hands in front of him. He studied them as if they held the answer to an ancient mystery. An answer to which only he was privy. "Beth Marshall for one."

"And?"

"T.R. Slone for two."

"And?"

"Les Johnson for three."

The way he answered made me wonder a little. Either he held all the cards and was toying with me, or there was a wild card still in the deck. I needed to know.

"What about Preston Marshall? He was also at the Coach House that evening."

Lethridge's eyes flicked away from his hands and lighted on my face. I glanced at his hands. If they were full of meaning, I couldn't see it.

"Think your old football buddy will cover for you?"

"No, but he might have seen something the others missed." It was a long shot across a dark night, but the only shot I had. I lifted my eyes and stared into Lethridge's. It felt like I was looking into a two-way mirror. Lethridge could see me, but I couldn't see him, not inside his brain anyway, which was where I needed to go.

"Don't think Mr. Marshall would risk his reputation for a drunken has-been facing a long stretch at Eddyville."

"So you haven't interviewed him yet?"

Lethridge stood up. He looked as lean and hard as a steel post. "Not yet. Mr. Marshall has a very busy schedule, but I'm sure the detectives will hook up with him soon." He made it sound like a threat.

Lethridge jerked his flat-planed face at Perkins. "Get him out of here. Mr. Kohler is not ready to be cooperative. Take him back to his cell until he is."

Meaty hands gripped both my arms. Perkins and Dunn felt like the angels of death. It was only my imagination, but Lethridge's eyes seemed to burn a hole in my back until the door clicked behind us.

Bastard made me feel guilty. And I was. Guilty of numerous sins. But not the liquor store holdup. If I hadn't been wide awake and sober I'd have sworn I was having a nightmare. Instead, I was living one. The three of us marched as one down the long hall shining like the pathway to heaven, only all the lights were artificial. My legs were trembling and I wanted to scream. I gnawed on my lip and kept marching.

24

Nights had never seemed so long. Nothing to drink, nothing to read, nothing to do. A battery of lights burned in the hall and one light, protected by wire mesh, remained on in our cell. Constant yellow glow created a surreal atmosphere, where it was never either quite light or quite dark. Call it Andy Warhol's version of Dante's *Inferno*.

Normally a private sort, after a couple of these nights I was lonely enough to talk. However, my cellmate possessed two wonderful abilities, even if he could do nothing much else right in the world, which to hear his story was how it was.

His two skills, which he demonstrated nightly, were a marvelous ability to drop off to sleep almost the instant he closed his eyes and a truly tremendous snoring technique. His snores were long and deep and loud, they sounded like a train whistle on steroids. He kept them up through the night, pausing only now and then as if to catch his breath.

I lay on my hard flat mattress and counted minutes as they made their agonizingly slow crawl toward morning. Nighttime also afforded the opportunity for some thoughtful introspection. After the first night, I tried to do as little thinking about myself and my situation as possible. Thinking about either one was as pointless as trekking across a barren wasteland. That much, I'd figured out.

It was one thing to waste your life; it was another to admit it, even to your private self. I wanted to go back and run all the plays again. Only there were just two minutes left and I was out of timeouts.

Horizontal on my lonely bed, I concocted a hundred different defenses and semi-plausible alibis that might help eradicate me from my current straits. However, I was able to poke holes in all my strategies with discouraging ease. If even an inept locker room lawyer could ventilate my alibis it made me shudder to think what the prosecutor would do.

One thing I could see quite clearly. Without corroborating witnesses it was going to be extremely difficult to prove that I hadn't done the liquor store hold-up. For hours I racked my brain, but could not recall more about that night after I left the Coach House than a foggy patchwork of vague, distorted images that danced at the periphery of my memory, never coming into the light. Something wasn't quite right about that night, but no matter how hard I tried I just couldn't figure out what.

Still, I just could not see me robbing a liquor store, or shooting anyone, not in my wildest nightmare. Nothing made sense. If the jail cell hadn't been so real I'd have sworn I'd slipped a cog. Maybe I had at that. There were times I wasn't quite sure who I was, or who I was becoming. Some nights, in that dead zone between midnight and daylight, I could almost feel myself becoming another man, a man whose name I did not know.

I stared at the stains on the ceiling and wondered how in the hell I had managed to fuck so much up. You could argue I'd accomplished a great deal in only a few years, unfortunately most of it was the sort of thing you wouldn't want your mother to find out. After cataloging my sins, I reflected on who I could blame for my current sad state of affairs, and while I was at it, the last dozen years.

My mother and father had treated me far better than I had ever treated them. It was not the fault of the coach who called someone else's number. Honestly, I couldn't blame the man who fired me at the bank because I failed to show up for two weeks, nor any of the women who left me because I loved alcohol more than them. It wasn't the first time I got blind-pig drunk, nor the twenty-third. Really no one to blame except myself. All that was history; I was braying against ghosts. I only drank to fill the emptiness, and to drown my shame. And who was responsible for those?

Smiling at the depths of my foolishness, I told myself I'd never drink another drop. I knew that was a lie. Already, I could feel the trembling. I spat on the floor and turned onto my side and stared at the smooth cool gray wall. A man who had lain in my bed before me had penned in neat letters: *What is the answer?* Below that, another had scrawled in pencil: *You are the answer, asshole, and also the question.* I felt a certain Sunday afternoon sympathy for both points of view. I felt a greater sympathy for myself. The nights were disgustingly long.

25

My cellmate was telling me for the third time about his no-account brother-in-law when the guard came. For once I was actually glad to see the uniform.

"I tell you, man, that dude is one lazy motherfucker. Makes his wife dance over at Camelot East, and then half the damn time makes her take a cab home. That is one sorry motherfucker when he won't go get his own woman and make sure she gets home safe. And she brings him plenty of jack, too. She is one fine looking woman—white, and big fat titties and slim legs. Dancer's legs, you know. Why, she brings in a couple of hundred every night she works, and that sorry prick makes her work six nights a week."

"Kohler." The guard's voice cut off my cellmate's ramblings. You know the times are bad when you're glad to hear the law call your name.

"Yeah."

"Time to take a walk."

I sat on the side of my bunk and put on my shoes without laces. Then I started shuffling. Walking with unlaced shoes is difficult. All the way across the narrow cell to where the guard waited with his finger on the big key pad I could feel the black man's eyes on me. He hadn't had a visitor since I'd been in the cell with him. Not even his lawyer.

I stepped through the open doorway and out into the hall. My shadow lengthened before me. "Dead Head again?"

"Who?" The guard walked close behind me. Another waited twenty feet down the well-lighted corridor.

"Captain Lethridge."

"No. You've got a visitor." The guard sounded envious.

This time we weren't in the community chat room. Instead, they escorted me to a small private room furnished with three straight-backed chairs and a Formica-topped table. As I crossed the linoleum I heard the door click behind me.

For several minutes I sat in one of the chairs and wondered. I wondered who wanted to see me. I wondered if I would ever get out of jail. I even wondered if the guards were secretly watching me from behind the two-way mirror that ran the length of one of the shorter walls. Then I began to wonder if I was going crazy.

I'd just about decided I was when the lock clicked and the door swung open to admit Preston Marshall, debonair in a two-piece, European cut, blue, pin-striped suit. His tie was a maze of silver swirls on a blue background. His hair was perfect and his smile too white to be real. Press crossed the room like an actor making an entrance, then sat in a chair directly across the table from me. He didn't offer to shake hands, which didn't hurt my feelings.

"Frank, how's it going?"

"Okay, for being in hell."

He put his elbows on the table and leaned forward. He gave me another smile. His teeth were incredibly white. I wondered if he had them painted. Then I tried to remember the last time I'd been to the dentist.

"I've got my attorney coming, but we need to talk first."

Now what was he up to, I wondered. I couldn't figure the play so I shrugged my shoulders. "Alright, let's talk."

"Quietly," he whispered, inclining his head toward me. There was no expression in his blue eyes I could read. I leaned forward until our faces were only inches apart.

"Talk about what?"

"Your situation," he whispered.

"What about it?"

"I've been making inquiries. Discreet ones. Doesn't look good."

"Tell me something I don't know."

"Everyone who has told their story puts you in a bad light."

I was confused; so far I couldn't figure out where Press was headed, but I didn't see how it would hurt to play along. "So Lethridge told me."

"He's a tough cop."

"That I believe."

"Also an honest one. Totally honest."

"Okay, so what?"

"So that makes it tough to work any sort of a deal." His whispers were so faint I had to strain to hear them.

"Deal, what kind of deal are you talking about?" Against my better judgment, I could feel excitement singing through my veins.

"One to get you out of here."

"Can you do that? How?"

"Won't be easy. I had a hell of a time arranging this private interview, had to pull some strings. But I got McChesney working on your case. He's one of the best." Press looked slowly around the room. "We have one card left to play."

"What's that?"

"My story."

"What do you mean?" A nerve jumped in my check.

"Everyone else says you never came back to the table after you left the last time."

"What about you?"

"I haven't been available for the Captain. Yet." His head came up and his blue eyes locked on mine. "If I say the same, you don't have a prayer of avoiding time."

He made caterpillars with his eyebrows. "The man is after me. I've got to become available soon, real soon." Press glanced around the room as though he expected Lethridge to materialize out of the air.

Nasty little suspicions were starting to stir in my brain. Press was calling a play, but I couldn't quite catch the signal. "But you don't have to say the same as everyone else?"

"That's right." His lips were close enough to my ear that I could feel the warmth of his breath. "I was gone from the table myself for quite a while that night. Had to make a couple of phone calls. I could say that you and I met up in the men's room and I walked you to your car, saw you were too drunk to drive and drove you home myself."

"Then how did you get back to the Coach House?"

"Let's say I called a friend, a very cooperative friend." He smiled all the way up to his eyes.

My hands were starting to shake. I put them in my lap. "Will it stand up?"

"I can make it stand. I can say I didn't leave you until an hour after the robbery." He paused and rubbed the back of his right hand over his mouth as if to erase the lie. His left eye twitched. "If…"

My left leg was bouncing up and down involuntarily and I pressed down on it with the sweaty palm of one hand. "If what?"

He gave me the gleaming white smile. It looked like a politician's smile. I decided if I ever got out I would vote only for candidates who didn't smile. Preston cleared his throat. "If you will help me out."

"How can I possibly help you out?" No part of this conversation was making sense. It was a disturbingly surreal exchange, like a few conversations I'd had when I was loaded.

"Will you do it?"

"Do I have a choice?"

Very faintly, as though peering through a thick, cold, river-bottom fog, I could see that if I agreed I'd be heading down a dark trail. More clearly, I could see that I didn't have any real choice. Not unless I wanted to spend one hell of a lot of years on the wrong side of the walls of the Kentucky State Penitentiary.

"I don't see one." Preston spoke quite matter-of-factly. He might have been reading a newspaper article aloud.

I closed my eyes and thought about a lot of things very quickly. Mostly, I thought about how I'd fucked up my life. I was getting tired of thinking about that. Truth was, I was starting to bore myself. Why didn't I change? Surely change couldn't be worse than the current reality. I opened my eyes. "Okay, I'll do it. What is it?"

Preston Marshall smiled again, a little more brightly. "Oh, nothing too difficult."

I closed my eyes again. I didn't trust them. They would have revealed too much. "Press, tell me what nothing too difficult is."

He sighed and scooted his chair closer to the table. Chair legs screeched against the floor. "Frank?"

"Yeah." I opened my eyes. A fine sheen of perspiration glistened on Preston's forehead. I fixed my gaze on the wall behind his head. Poker was never my game.

"I am a man in a particular position." His voice was soft.

"What position?"

"For the past five years I've worked diligently and put myself in the public eye. Next year there will be an election for U.S. Senator. The incumbent is old, feeble, and half senile, but he has a lot of power, not to mention many excellent connections. I plan to run. However, with my handicap I can't win."

"What handicap?" I could hear the surprise in my voice.

He whispered one word. Whispered it so low that I wasn't sure I understood him. The word didn't make sense. I glanced at his face. If there was an expression there I couldn't read it.

I whispered back. "Beth?"

"Yes. After Clinton, a man has to have an impeccable family life. As you know, Beth drinks. Drinks to excess some might say. My opponent, the incumbent, and his henchmen will say worse." He swallowed. I watched his Adam's apple go up and down.

"You can help me, and Beth. She's been under a lot of strain lately. All the pressures of being in the public eye only make her drink more. She's miserable." He looked me directly in the eyes. I refused to let myself blink.

"Beth needs a vacation. You could take her to Mexico, show her a good time, party a bit."

"Wouldn't your opponent make an issue of us being together?"

"You are old friends, dinner companions, best man at my wedding. Les and his girlfriend can go with you. Then he can make an unexpected early return."

"So then, just a little vacation to Mexico for a couple of weeks?"

He paused with his mouth half-open. In the still, sterile room I could hear our breathing. We were out of synch.

"Then what?" I asked. I didn't understand where my old teammate was headed. Never had been good at guessing games.

"Then you repay all your debts."

Primitive wigglings, like primeval worms, at the bottom of my brain told me I didn't want to know the answer. But there was no choice now; I had to know. "How, Press?"

"Just one little accident. So tragic, so final." His voice was a whisper of a whisper.

"What do you mean, an accident?" It was one of those questions you really don't want to ask, but know you'd better.

"Just that, Frank." In my ear, his voice was abrupt and hard as nails. "I tell my story, our version, to Lethridge and you arrange a little accident for Beth south of the border. Only you make damn sure it's a fatal one."

I wanted to avert my gaze from his eyes, but I couldn't. I just kept staring. Staring and sweating. True, I was a worthless bastard, but not that bad. Surely. I felt the walls were closing around me.

"Deal? Or do you want to spend the next twenty years behind bars at Eddyville with the animals?"

I swallowed hard. "Give me some time to think." My mind felt like it was melting. Coming apart at the seams like Dali's clocks.

"No, Frank. It's now or never. Agree to do this for me, and I'll make sure you go free. Pass, and it is a one way ticket to the state penitentiary. And don't think you can run an end-around on me with Lethridge. He would never believe your story over mine. Not in a million years."

His smile transformed into a smirk. "Lots of big, black fellows will enjoy having some fine, fresh, white meat. Now we don't want that, do we?" He looked down at the palms of his hands. Then his eyes came back to my face. "What's your answer, Frank? It's now, or never."

My brain felt like it was rupturing. I needed a drink. I wanted to scream. I shut my eyes and tried to shut down the bubbling surface of my brain. Part of me couldn't believe what I was hearing. Worse, part of me was thinking hard about what Press had said. My pulse hammered at my temples. There had to be a way out, only I couldn't see it just yet.

Time was what I needed. Time and distance and maybe I could alter the equation. I tried to think, but the river of thoughts had gone dry. Still, I had to make a play. The game was down to the final seconds and I could hear the clock ticking. My stomach hurt. My brain hurt worse.

After what seemed like a very long time, I heard myself say, "Okay, you bastard. Now get me out of here, and get me a drink." The voice seemed to come from far away. It was as though a stranger had spoken. My head felt hollow. Never had I despised myself more.

"Good deal, compadre." His knee nudged mine under the table. "Knew I could count on you, so I brought you something to celebrate with. Just open your hand."

A small glass bottle slid against my palm. The glass felt smooth. Smooth glass was one of my favorite things to feel. Cupping the bottle I drank the half-pint in three hard swallows and palmed the bottle back to Press.

A stray thought wandered a back trail in my mind. Maybe I could drink myself to death before I hit the Mexican border.

26

Fifty-two hours and seventeen minutes later I was sitting in an aisle seat on a Delta 747 staring down the main runway at Blue Grass Airport. Beth sat in the seat beside me. We had each downed two cocktails in the lounge before boarding. Neither of us was feeling any pain as the plane began to roll.

Lately, I'd been encountering a number of random thoughts and just then another wandered unbidden across my mind. Captain Lethridge was probably feeling something, and it wasn't pain either. Last time our paths had crossed his face had been dark with anger. He was furious at Preston for giving me an alibi, furious at me for going free, and furious with himself for being unable to stop the freedom train.

"If it's the last thing I do I'll get you, Kohler," he had told me as I waited for my attorney.

"Ever occur to you, Captain, that I might be innocent?" I'd asked him.

"All things are possible," he'd said through gritted teeth. Then he'd added, "But if you are guilty, I'll get you, even if it takes ten years. If you're not, so be it. I'll just have to find whoever really did it. And don't think I won't."

He'd made a fist and then unclenched. "Know this, Kohler, until I'm satisfied that you truly are innocent, be prepared to see my face every time you turn around. I'll be there when you least expect it. Long after you think I've forgotten about you, you'll see something out the corner of your eye and it will be me. If there's one thing I hate, it's to see some guilty bastard go free."

"Lethridge, I tell you, I'm innocent."

"Keep telling yourself that, you drunken shit. Do it long enough and you might even start to believe it."

Berson McChesney, Preston's attorney, had come then and hurried me to the door. Twenty yards down the long, white sidewalk I'd looked back. Lethridge was still there, standing in the doorway shading his eyes with one hand against the sunlight.

The plane was picking up speed and the pilot got the nose up and we started to rise. Leaning across Beth, I glanced out the window. Small knots of people stood on the observation deck following our progress. Probably my imagination, but one of them put me in mind of Lethridge.

27

A breeze worked its way across the sandy spit and through the copse of trees. The air was so soft and full of fragrance that it seemed alive. I lay on a canvas and aluminum chaise lounge with my eyes closed and tried to imagine living permanently in such a climate.

Suddenly another odor drifted into my nostrils, strong and fresh and acrid. I opened my eyes to find Les puffing on a dark cigar the size of a Mexican banana.

Les's girlfriend, Marcia, wrinkled her nose. "Phew, put that nasty thing out."

She inched her slim, ebony body against the railing as if to physically distance herself from the smoke.

"No way, woman. This is a good smoke."

"Now that is an oxymoron if ever I heard one."

Les snorted through his nose. He sounded like a slightly plastered bull elephant. "You wouldn't know an oxymoron if one bit you on your cute little ass."

Marcia straightened her back and let her lips drift back from unnaturally white teeth.

"Les Johnson, you are positively vulgar when you have been drinking. What do you think your friends think about us?"

Les took a drag off the cigar and made his mouth emit a small cloud of purplish gray smoke in her direction. "Frank don't care, do you Frank?"

"Not me."

Les turned his head toward the other side of the second floor veranda. "What about you, Beth? You mind if I enjoy a few brief moments of pleasure with a fine after-dinner cigar?"

Beth looked up sleepily, her nearly empty after-dinner Margarita cupped in her hands. It was her third. She was wearing a two piece terry cloth shorts set and her top had ridden up over her tummy. Rolls of fat hung down each side and the flab of her inner thighs jiggled as she shifted in her recliner. Hard to believe that she'd ever been a college cheerleader. "What did you say, Les?"

"Asked if you were grossly offended by my smoking?"

"No," she said in a thick voice, "I don't care. Whatever you want to do is fine with me."

She lifted her glass to her lips and took a long swallow. I admired her long and still beautiful neck.

"Right now all I care about is another drink. Marcia, you want to go get another one with me?"

"Sure, honey. Let's get out of here and let these two old has-been football players tell each other lies and catch cancer from that damn nasty cigar."

Marcia leaned forward and helped Beth who was struggling to escape from her chair. "Come on, Mrs. Marshall. Just hold onto my arm."

They moved across the veranda in a mistimed tango, a young, model-thin black girl leading a middle-aged white woman, who was growing plumper and drunker by the glass. Beth needed a full-time keeper. Easy to see why Preston wanted a change.

At the door, Marcia turned her head and said out of the corner of her mouth, "Les, you and your nasty cigar breath can just sleep on the couch tonight."

Les chuckled, the sound rumbling deep in his chest. "Don't worry, witch, as long as there are senoritas around Les Johnson don't ever have to sleep alone."

The black girl jerked her head around, pointed her nose in the air, and helped her companion up the single step and into the room. I watched them until they rounded the corner and slid behind a pink adobe wall. With each step Beth's buttocks bounced up and down like miniature basketballs. She wasn't wearing any underwear.

Les took another puff off his cigar and let smoke roll out of the corner of his mouth. "Remember what tomorrow is, Frank?"

"What's that?"

"Tomorrow, Frank."

"Yeah?"

Les shook his head. It looked like a bowling ball working its way through a smoke screen. "I got a phone call tonight, from Kentucky."

"Oh, okay." Now I knew where he was headed.

"Yeah, okay. That phone call means old Les and his lovely companion pull out of here tomorrow. You and Mrs. Preston Marshall will have to spend the rest of your vacation without benefit of our invigorating company." He chuckled. These days Les Johnson thought he was very funny. I found him less so every day.

"Understand what goes down next?"

I took a drink, a long one. "Yeah."

Les chuckled again. "Don't sound so happy about it, Frank."

"I'm not."

"You got a job to do. Just do it." His voice had taken on a serious tone.

"I will."

"Press and I are counting on you."

I heard the threat, running like a steel rail just below the surface of the words. "I won't let you down."

"Good. Told Press we could count on you."

I turned and leaned across the rail, peering at the blackness that seemed to grow directly from the jungle. Below the courtyard was quiet. To my right a trio of palms swayed softly. Soft moths, the size of my hand, fluttered silently against yellow bug lights. I could hear Les stirring in his chair.

"Frank." His voice was softer, pitched deliberately low.

"Yeah."

"Read a factoid in the *Herald-Leader* just before we left Lexington."

"What was that?" I asked, wondering if I really wanted to know the answer.

"More fatal accidents happen in the home than anywhere else."

The wind was changing and I could smell the acrid smoke of his cigar. It burned in my nostrils. "Is that right?"

"Sure enough."

I was right. I hadn't wanted to know the answer.

Time for a fresh drink.

Time for a little pain killer.

Time for a sliver of oblivion.

28

In the glory days of rock and roll—before the pabulum known as Pop pervaded and poisoned the purity of the primitive sound—some group, I think it was the Essex, had a hit song called, "Easier Said Than Done." I woke up in a cold sweat at four in the morning realizing that my Mexican mission was going to be a lot like the song.

It's one thing to say you will do something evil and wicked, even to believe at the time that you can and will. Undeniably another to actually perform the deed. Back in Lexington we'd talked about ways. Preston favored a fall in the bathtub and let the maid find her. Les voted for a quick tumble, late at night, off the twelfth floor of a building that was a combination observation deck and helicopter pad. He figured that by the time someone located and responded to the splat I'd be back in my own room under the covers.

Both plans had merit. Also problems. Beth's now almost complete inability to leave liquor alone had resulted in numerous drunken public appearances and one nasty fall in the hotel dining room. The fact that she capped the fall by promptly regurgitating the entire contents of her evening meal all over the maître d' put the punctuation point on that memorable evening.

Memories by the staff of these embarrassments would lend credence to a fatal fall theory. However, the heliport location was exposed. I'd taken an exploratory excursion and it seemed doable, but chancy.

My major concern was a security camera. These days most hotels were overbooked with them. A daylight survey hadn't uncovered one, yet a nagging doubt persisted in the back of my brain. Perhaps, I thought, it was like having someone on the other side of a two-way mirror; I couldn't see the camera, but the camera could record me.

Exposure for one Frank Kohler was my chief concern regarding the bathtub set up. That, and the fact that the technique had been done to death. In the past six months I'd seen two movies where the hard ceramic tub was the murderer's weapon of choice.

On top of that, all it would take was one lost guest or wandering bellboy in the wrong place at the wrong time and Señor Kohler was identified as leaving the room of the late Mrs. Marshall in great haste.

For the next two days I racked my brain while keeping Beth company and my throat well lubricated. Nothing brilliant occurred to me, but I did get a nice sunburn sitting around the pool.

Beth liked to lie in her chair and admire the slim-hipped, dark-skinned men. None had any interest in a drunken, overweight, middle-aged white woman. Several of the bikini clad señoras gave me glances accompanied by sad shakes of the head.

By the third day following Les's departure, desperation was beginning to set in. I had no ideas and damn little time. Our return trip plane tickets were for the day after next. Stress spawned stress until it saturated my brain and I couldn't think, except about what would happen to me if I failed. I thought about writing the whole story down and mailing it to a *Herald-Leader* beat writer I knew from my UK days, but it all seemed too much effort. Much easier to sit in the sun, listen with half an ear to Beth's all but incoherent ramblings, feel sorry for myself, and drown my sorrows in Mexican beer from short, dark-glass bottles. Just as the sun was bleeding to death against the western horizon, I got my idea; my grandly glorious, set me free why don't you babe, wonderfully wicked idea.

After an elongated afternoon of hard drinking, Beth had passed out and I was alone with my thoughts. End-of-the-day shadows, that grew longer with each passing moment, had marched across the lush green triangle that formed the end of the compound. A narrow concrete pathway ran from the swimming pool, down the hillside, until it terminated against the brown beach that afforded guests of Inca Shores sandy access to the ocean.

Deep and dark here, the Pacific was full of the promise of adventure, and danger, if one ventured too far from shore. The beach was set in a natural curve of the rocky coastline, with points of land jutting right and left of the inverted sandy crescent. Jagged rocks, breached now and then by scrubby pine and native bushes, marked the perimeter of the beach.

Twin points of land, like horns from the head of a Brahma bull, curled away from the beach at both ends, creating a small natural bay that offered fine swimming close to shore. Farther out, there was good water for sailing or wind surfing. I'd overheard some of the younger set discussing Hobe-Cats. A couple of sport-fishing boats anchored just offshore, and a poster in the lobby advertised diving and snorkeling. For the less adventuresome, primarily family groups with young children and nervous mothers, the natives rented a small boat that looked like a cross between a canoe and a flat-bottom rowboat. These drifted with the current or were propelled by paddles or oars.

The last sunlight of the day was burnishing the water when I heard a man yell. He was standing at the end of the short dock that jutted out into the bay midway down the right, or northernmost, point of land. He was gesturing at a family, who had apparently rented one of his boats, to come in.

From my vantage point it looked as if they were sincerely trying. A woman held two young children tightly against her body. The man and two older boys, who looked about eleven and thirteen, were paddling furiously. They appeared to have floated beyond the natural barriers, and the wind and tides were working against them. Despite their efforts, the small boat kept drifting farther out into deep blue water that ran all the way to Japan.

High and shrill, the woman's screams soared above the sounds of waves and wind. Suddenly she stood up and in that instant the balance was upset and the boat tipped over. Heads and arms bobbed above the whitecaps like truncated sea creatures.

From one end of the dock the man shouted again and a skinny old man ran barefoot down toward the other. There, hanging from a wooden beam that extended over the water, was a large iron bell. The old man pulled vigorously on the rope that dangled like a manila snake from the bell. The clang of the bell reverberated against the bluff and echoed around the bay.

Now more men were shouting. Some ran toward moored boats. Most of the people in the pool area were running down the slope toward the beach. Only an Englishman with a broken leg, a woman from Steubenville, Ohio who was too fat to get out of her sagging beach chair without help, and Beth, who snored with ladylike gentility, kept me company.

Once in the boats the men were quick and efficient. In less than five minutes they had picked up all of the dunked boaters. Men from a matching pair of blue, wooden boats stayed out beyond the calm water, struggling to right the overturned craft.

Suddenly it was easy to see that all I needed to do was drift with the tide far enough to be out of sight before the accident occurred. Then there would be no clanging bells and quick men in fast boats.

Beth had never taken a single dip in the pool or the ocean the entire time we'd been at Inca Shores. I wondered if she could even swim. Not that the question mattered. Enough alcohol, amplified by a blow to the head with a wooden boat paddle, would render the question academic. With an almost scientific abstraction, I noted that my stomach had suddenly gone queasy and my left leg trembled involuntarily.

The man with the broken leg was listening, with more patience that I possessed, to the fat Steubenville housefrau moan about her chair and the rudeness of the other guests. Beth had rolled over on her side so that she faced me. Fading sunlight tinted her face. Her full lips were parted, so that she seemed to be smiling to herself even as she continued to snore gently. A line of freckles marched down her chest, split, then climbed the rising swells of her breasts. Thinking about what I had to do made me want to cry; whether for her or for myself I wasn't sure. But I was a big boy, so I pushed myself out of my chair and went in search of a drink. Even a temporary oblivion would be welcome.

29

It was a night that didn't have a clue how to end.

Maybe I'd stopped drinking too soon in the afternoon. Perhaps I had bad shellfish for supper. Maybe it was my guilty conscience. If you could sin based on what was in your heart, witness President Jimmy Carter who once confessed to lust in *Playboy*, then I was damned for eternity.

In Kentucky, she'd made me sick with her drunken slutiness and public intoxication. In Mexico, she seemed more little girl lost. I sat in an overstuffed chair in my dark room and wondered whether it was she or I who had changed. Now I was certain of only one thing; I had no desire to keep my promise. Alone in a soft, enveloping darkness, I sat listening to the music and laughter drifting up from the courtyard and cantina below, trying to figure a way out.

My Spanish was rudimentary, but I understood songs of happy love and peaceful villages and a land where the sun shone forever. When the music stopped and the laughter died, I slipped off all my clothes and lay down, unwashed and naked on clean, white sheets. For some time I simply lay there thinking about the man I'd become and what I was going to do and was it truly too late for me to turn my life around. Nothing I could think of gave me any solace, but somewhere in the curve of the night I drifted off.

30

"Do you like it?"

Beth twirled on her toes in a sleeveless blue dress sprinkled with pinpoints of silver. In the right light it would look like hundreds of stars flung against the night sky. In the harsh sunlight of Mexico she looked like a bulked up ballerina coming off an overlong road tour.

"Very nice."

We were lazing on the patio jutting from her room. I was sipping black coffee that was as strong and hot as the sunlight burning the back of my neck.

"It's a new one. I've never worn it before. Bought it before we left Lexington." Excitement vibrated in her voice. A smile tap-danced across her lips.

"Looks good on you," I lied. It was too tight across her plump stomach and spreading hips, and her upper arms had gone too flabby for the sleeveless look.

Beth walked across the narrow patio and leaned over my shoulder. Her shadow darkened my newspaper. "Your coffee good?"

"Strong."

"Frank?"

"Yes."

She put her chin on my shoulder. Her perfume smelled like a basketful of flowers.

"Are you having a good time?"

"Sure. You?"

"Mexico is wonderful. I haven't had this good a time in years. Think we could stay a little longer?" Her voice had gone all little girl. I hated when she did that. That voice worked on me. Only I couldn't let it. I had a promise to keep.

I sipped coffee and did some quick reconnoitering. She had given me my cue; I wanted to be sure I played it right.

"Well, that would be nice, but our airplane tickets are already set."

"You could get them changed, or buy new ones."

"That would cost more money than I have. Besides, you have a husband at home."

"Press? He wouldn't miss me. Some days he doesn't even know I'm there. Sometimes I think he wouldn't care if I disappeared and never came back."

I forced a chuckle to cover my surprise at her perception. She must not have been totally blinded by the alcoholic haze.

"Wish we could make a change, but, since we can't, you want to do something special this afternoon?"

"Sure. What do you have in mind?"

"How about a boat ride down the coast? The natives have some nice little craft we can rent. Just the two of us. Very Mexican. Drift with the tides, then put ashore and have a picnic. How does that sound?"

She hugged my neck. "Frank, that sounds wonderful. When can we go?"

"I'll go soon and make the arrangements with the boat people. Why don't you call the hotel kitchen and have them fix us some lunch to take along. Just tell them to put it on the bill."

"Great. I'll go do it right now." She skipped across the porch like a teenager, then paused with one foot already in her room. "Can I wear my new dress?"

"Sure, Beth. Anything you like." As a last wish it wasn't much.

Actually, a blue shroud sounded quite nice. I took a final sip of my coffee. It had turned bitter. I wondered if death tasted that bitter.

31

Giggling like a schoolgirl on a field trip, Beth held my left hand as we walked down to the dock. In my right I carried the picnic basket the kitchen had packed. The sky was a hard blue.

Only a light breeze blew in from the ocean. Long before we reached the dock sweat was rolling down my back. Tiny beads stood out in a row above Beth's upper lip, but otherwise she seemed unaffected. Maybe her sleeveless dress had been a good idea.

As we stepped onto the dock two dark-skinned men came out from a long, low shed. One was about fifty, short, balding, and turning to fat. The other was younger, taller, and slimmer. Muscles in his bare arms stood out like corded rope. A cigarette hung from the corner of his thin, hard mouth.

The older man stepped forward and greeted us with the smile he saved for the tourists.

"*Buenos dios*, Señor. Have you come about a boat for you and your señorita?"

I nodded. "Sí, from the hotel." At the moment I was not in the mood for Latin courtesies. What I needed was a boat and a drink, not necessarily in that order.

"Will you need a boat for just the afternoon?"

"Yes."

"*Bueno*. Then you will need to have the boat back to us by eight. That is when we close for the evening."

"Works for us, but what if we're late?" I winked at him.

He looked like a man who would hold a soft spot in his heart for lovers, even lovers who were no longer young and beautiful.

He gave me a furtive smile. "Then Pedro or I will wait. But not too late, Señor, or there might be a late fee."

"I understand. How much for the boat?"

He told me and I handed him a fistful of American dollars. As he counted them he gave rapid fire instructions to Pedro who sauntered to the nearest slip where he untied a small, blue boat. The cigarette still dangled from his lips and smoke curled around his sleek dark head.

As we walked across the dock the older man gave me my receipt, chatting all the way with Beth. They talked about the weather, the water, and whether Mexican women wore more pants or dresses. I just listened; small talk was on the agenda for the afternoon.

He helped us into the boat while Pedro stood by holding the picnic basket. The sullen look in his eyes spilled over and ran down the sharp planes of his face. After Beth and I were safely aboard, the older man retrieved the basket from Pedro. As he leaned over to hand it to me he made eye contact.

"Señor."

"Yes."

"Take care, especially of your lovely lady. I have the gift, and I can see that she is very special." He smiled broadly, but there were only serious lights in his eyes. "The wind is picking up and the signs speak of storms."

"I'll be careful, amigo." The blue sky seemed to belie his warning.

He laughed, short and hard, then he and Pedro gave the boat a shove. The tide quickly began to pull the vessel away from the dock toward the south. Beth and I had little trouble manning the boat in the calm water of the bay.

When we were about thirty yards away from the dock I looked back. The old man and Pedro were still standing at the edge of the slip looking silently in our direction, their faces closed like shelved books, impossible to read.

Sunlight danced on the blue surface. The little boat moved easily, drifting in a current that grew stronger as we neared the point. The boat was equipped with a small electric trolling motor, as well as an ancient Evinrude, but the drift of the ocean suited us.

In half an hour we'd rounded the point and were out of sight of both the hotel and the beach, although, when the wind faltered, we could hear an occasional squeal of laughter.

As we drifted south we moved away from the hotel and its landscaped grounds. Carefully manicured lawn and trimmed shrubbery gave way to unkempt undergrowth, and thin, dark trees that seemed too exhausted after their fight through the undergrowth to attain significant height.

Beth lay in the prow of the boat, soaking up sunlight and sipping on a glass bottle of water. I sat at the other end between motors and gasoline cans, where the smell of fish mixed with the odor of gasoline. Fish scales, dried by untold hours in the sun, clung stubbornly to the wooden sides of the boat. The blue paint was beginning to flake and chip. I drank Negra Modelo just starting to go warm.

We drifted, chatting occasionally but mostly silent, each wrapped in our own thoughts. Beth smiled often and from time to time trailed a soft white hand in the water. Sporadically, she flipped water at me.

Almost imperceptibly the wind began to pick up, forcing us gently but firmly toward the rocks. I started the trolling motor to keep us away from the shore. By mid-afternoon, with no substantial breakfast in my stomach, I began to feel a few hunger pangs, or perhaps it was nerves. Beth had been quiet for several minutes, but when I shifted positions her eyes opened and she smiled at me. Reclining at the far end of the boat, she looked inexplicably young. I couldn't figure out why, unless it was that silky blue dress.

"Getting hungry?" I asked.

"A little."

"You want me to put into shore so we can have our picnic? There's a flat rock that would make a good table."

"Frank?"

"What?"

She sat up straight, curves rising and falling beneath her blue dress. "It's so wonderful out here in the boat, just drifting along. Would you mind terribly if we just had our picnic out here?"

I thought for a second. "Okay."

"Good." As she reached for the basket a shadow of a passing cloud drifted across us, spreading its fingers darkly across the blue waters.

She handed me a cardboard box. It contained a thick ham sandwich, a bag of chips, an apple, a banana, and three chocolate chip cookies that looked homemade. A man could live for days on such rations.

The wind was rising now, whistling to herself. White caps were beginning to pop up before us. I turned my head. Fifty yards away, wave action, clearly more substantial than before, was visible. The blue sky was pock-marked with dark clouds advancing from the west.

Beth munched on her lunch, smiling shyly at me between bites. The wind was sharp in my ears now and my sandwich tasted like stale sawdust.

In half an hour the breeze had freshened noticeably and the current was stronger. The little trolling motor was no longer sufficient and I began to fiddle with the Evinrude. White caps were pronounced, slapping urgently against the side of the boat. Water sloshed over the sides each time we turned into a swell.

"It's getting dark. Is there a storm coming?" Beth's eyes were fixed on a sky mottled with dark gray clouds. Her eyes appeared darker too, as if they were undergoing a sea change.

"Don't know. Didn't listen to the radio before we left, but I wouldn't be surprised."

Beth began to get busy securing the picnic items. Her eyes flicked to mine. "Frank, think we ought to head back?"

I shrugged, feigning more indifference than I felt. The wind was changing, growing by the minute. There was a nasty taste in my mouth. I wasn't sure if it was fear or disgust. Whichever it was, I swallowed it.

"Maybe we should. Why don't you finish storing things away while I have a go at the motor."

"Okay." She smiled at me with a cheerfulness I wished I felt. It's one thing to feel like a bastard. Quite another to be one.

I took a peek at my watch. Twenty after four. We'd been drifting for a couple of hours. I really had no idea how far we'd traveled or how long it would take to get back to the dock. Looking toward the land, I could see sheer rock walls that jutted from a thick, somber forest into the water. There was little beach to speak of, and what there was looked narrow and rock strewn. As far as I could see there was no life of any kind; no birds, no animals, no man, no woman, no child. About a hundred yards to the north the rocks made a stronger foray into the ocean, a jumbled barricade that extended forty or fifty yards into the water. With the rising sea it would take a strong swim, but in all other ways the conditions were perfect. Now or never.

I stood up quickly and began to jerk at the starter cord of the Evinrude. Hatred rose in my throat, choking me. I coughed and spat and silently cursed; first God, then Preston Marshall, and finally myself. I had sold my soul for a half-pint and a taste of freedom. I longed to be anywhere in the world but in the small boat. I tried to tell myself I didn't have to do this, that I could just disappear in the jungles of Mexico. Making myself believe it was another matter.

Guilt and loathing flowed through me and I jerked on the cord with a fury. Somehow it seemed appropriate that the gas line was unhooked and floating in the saltwater like the tail of a serpent. As the first hard barrage of rain pelted sharply against our faces, I jerked on the starter cord again.

Beth shouted but I couldn't understand her words above the wind driven rain. She was crouched in the prow of the boat, her shoulders scrunched up and head tucked down tight against her chest. I leaned toward her.

"What did you say?"

"I said, what's the matter? Won't it start?" Even with the rain and wind the fear in her voice was easy to detect.

"No. Something seems wrong with the gas line."

"My God, Frank, what are we going to do?"

"Stay calm. There's a point of land just ahead." I pointed at the rocks. "I'm going to try and work us in that direction."

"Hurry, Frank." Beth's eyes flicked to the rocks, then back to my face. Her mouth opened as if she wanted to speak, but she didn't make a sound.

"I'm hurrying. Just hold on. Only a few more yards and we'll start to get some shelter from the rocks. We're going to make it."

One of us is anyway, I silently added. I was a damn good liar. I made myself want to puke.

Beth nodded and tried to smile. It was a thin-lipped, shaky smile, and it made me sick to think it would be her last. I told myself I should jump in and drown my sorry self; I knew I didn't have the guts.

Wind and tide sent us careening toward rocks looming huge and black and wet before us. In the driving rain they looked like a crumbling medieval European fortress. We were close enough that I could make out individual boulders and low scrubby trees. Thirty to forty yards were left in our run. I began to make my move.

Beth was shouting at me, but I heard only my name. Wind was whipping in my ears and my face was awash. I couldn't seem to quite catch my breath. My muscles felt like old elastic that had lost its snap.

I began to wonder if I could do it. I knew what Press would do if I didn't. I could almost hear Lethridge's voice in the growl of the wind. I told myself I had to do it. I told myself I couldn't do it. Chilling rain hammered against my face. I wanted to scream.

I never saw the shelf of rock just below the surface. The boat shuddered as the hull stuck the rock. Beth screamed and I felt myself flung into the air.

Something far harder than water smashed against my head and the world began to spin black. The smell of blood was in my nostrils. I had a fleeting vision of myself as a small boy running hard through a meadow of grass as tall as my waist, trying to catch cloud shadows. Then the water pulled me under and I tasted salt, flavored with blood. An immense roaring filled my ears. Just before the world faded to black I had a sudden urge to laugh at myself. In trying to cause Beth's death I had arranged my own. Not understanding precisely why, I said her name. Perhaps it was penance.

32

Blood filled my mouth and I couldn't breathe. Sand filled my eye sockets and I was blind. I could feel heat on my face, but faintly, as if it were borne from a distant, dying sun.

Death was strange, not at all what I had imagined. No gold-fringed clouds of bliss. No fingers of fire. Neither heaven nor hell, but some indiscernible, indefinable, nether region.

I floated above my wasted body, cast haphazardly ashore on a deserted Mexican beach, the sun directly above, pouring through the clouds, burning my face. I was a dwarf, a midget, an insect shell of a man, an infinitesimal fragment of inconsequential organic matter shrouded in thick, heavy, wet sand and trapped outside a battered, broken body, seeking entry back into my body.

Then I felt my lifeless body carried on a giant wall of water that rose above all the land that lay before it and swept across the shore, the flatlands, and the mountains.

I burned from a fire within. I froze from the evil, numbing cold of eternity. I was consumed by a fetid sludge of love and hate, sin and retribution, longing and fulfillment. I laughed. I cried. I lived a thousand lives. I died a thousand deaths. I was one with the universe. I was alone in deep space. There was light. There was darkness. There was everything. There was nothing.

Suddenly, without warning, I was enveloped by the presence of a pure, transcendental essence. Then, there was the exquisite loneliness known only by the dead, the dying, and the broken-hearted.

33

An anvil pressed against my heart while a butterfly waltzed across my lips. I played with the contrasts in my mind, tossing them back and forth like tennis balls across a gray net of woven synapses.

Light began to play at the corner of my left eye and I felt the right jerk sporadically. Someone called my name. Wings of wind caught it and carried it swiftly past me to a point so far away that I could no longer hear the word, nor know its meaning.

Slowly, like the birth of reluctant spring, a great warmth began to envelope my face. Flesh grew warmer until I felt that I must combust or melt. Air in my lungs now seemed to come from a blast furnace. In the distance a great bell tolled solemnly in muted, measured tones.

I came awake like an abandoned child, afraid to view the morning. I could not fathom where I was, or why I was there.

I lay on my back in damp brown sand and stared at a sky streaked with yellow. By stages, I became aware of something warm and wet at the corner of my mouth. I ran my tongue around my lips and tasted blood.

Off to my left there was movement. I could hear something slogging toward me through thick wet sand. I tried to raise my head but it was heavy, broken.

"So, Frank Kohler, you decided to live."

I tried to speak, but there were no sounds. I swallowed, tasting blood and sand. I tried again. "So it seems."

Beth must have been just out of view. Her hand fluttered on my forehead, soft and cool. "How badly are you hurt?"

"Don't know. My insides feel all mashed up and my head hurts like hell, but I don't think anything is broken."

"Can you sit up?"

"Let me try. Slowly." And slowly was how I did it. That took all I had and left me sweat-soaked and shaking.

"God, Frank, it's good to see you alive. You've got a bad cut right at the hairline. I bandaged it the best I could with a piece of my dress."

"Thanks. Damn, Beth, that was one hell of a blow."

"It came up so quickly."

Moving like an old man, I turned my head and looked up and down the narrow, brown beach. As far as I could see there was wet sand, dense rock, odd bits of flotsam and jetsam. Faded blue paint decorated a few shards of damp wood. The bottom of our picnic basket was wedged in a crevice between two jagged, brown boulders the size of a Volkswagen Beetle. Ten yards away a single tennis shoe stood upright on the sand. Idly, I wondered whose it was.

I looked into Beth's eyes. They were exactly the same color as the boat's paint. "Looks like the boat is gone," I said.

She nodded, damp hair clinging to her round face. "It must have smashed up on the rocks."

Her face was smudged, and sand still clung to her hair, but there was no blood, no bruising, no brokenness. Beyond her lay the western sky, no more than a thin crimson line. The storm had passed. Her eyes were alight and alive and her lips were parted and she looked lovely.

The sky was growing steadily darker. Only that single slat of light flowed from low on the western horizon. "It'll be dark soon," I said. "We don't have any matches."

"It may be a long cold night," she said. "Come here and we'll stay together for warmth."

The softness of her body seeped through damp clothes. I snuggled closer.

"Frank?"

"Yes."

"They'll look for us in the morning, won't they?"

"First light," I said to assure her. Unfortunately, I had no words of reassurance for myself. Holding her against my body I knew I couldn't fulfill my promise to Press. In granting her pardon I'd signed my own death warrant. I shivered in the light evening breeze. I was grateful for the fast closing darkness. It wouldn't wash away my sins, but it would cover the lies in my eyes.

34

Just before dawn I awoke, shivering. There was a dampness to the air. The tide was out and dark sand was firm beneath my feet. I left Beth sleeping on the sand and walked to the water's edge, muscles protesting every step. My insides felt like a single, massive bruise. Early morning sounds of birds accompanied me. It was too dark to see the birds.

Waves lapped against the shore. Listening closely, in the special stillness that is morning, I could pick up rhythms of the tide. My own breathing began to rise and fall in sympathy.

I could make out profiles of rocks. Mist obscured their peaks. Over my shoulder the sun was transforming itself into a pale yellow disc.

What I couldn't see was a way out. My lies had turned back on themselves like snakes striking their own tails. With the first true light parties from the dock and the resort would be on the water. They would find us within the hour; unless...

I wanted a drink very badly. One would clear my head. Two would prime the pump. Three would start the engine. I didn't even have water, and I knew it. That didn't make me want a drink any less. I stood lusting for a drink, driving myself to think. Decisions I made in the next few minutes would be critical. One more good lie was all I needed. Maybe that was my philosophy of life. Funny where you are when the great revelations come.

When I could see tiny fish swimming in the tidal pools, I turned and walked back to Beth. The birds were visible now. Three of them were perched on the peaks of three successive boulders. The middle boulder rose higher than the others. Bright yellow bird eyes followed me all the way to Beth.

"Beth, wake up." I shook her shoulder gently.

She sat upright, a child's look of surprise on her face. "What's the matter, Frank? Something wrong?"

"Nothing is wrong. We just need to talk. It'll be full daylight soon."

"That's good, isn't it? They will come then, won't they?"

"Probably. That's what we need to talk about."

She brought her eyes up to mine. I couldn't make myself look at them.

"Know this is a hell of a time to spring this on you, but I'm in a fix."

"What kind of fix?"

"Back home I made a few enemies. Sort of planned all along to blend into the countryside here. Pull the old disappearing act, you know. Well, I got word yesterday that the guys I'd pissed off were closing in on me. When my name pops up at the top of the missing list at the hotel they'll be in the vanguard of the rescue team. Only these guys won't be there to save anybody."

"But..."

"Hush and listen to me. Back in the states I did some stupid things. They were wrong and I knew I'd have to pay someday. Only not this soon and not this much."

"Frank..."

"Listen, Beth." Morning sunlight was warm enough now to pop sweat out across the back of my neck. I knew now that I could never try to kill Beth again. However, staying where we were wasn't a viable option. Not unless I wanted to sign my own death warrant. I began to talk faster and help Beth out of the sand at the same time.

"Only reason I'm still alive is that they thought I was going to do one more job for them, and I was. Only the damn storm messed everything up and now it looks like I've run out on them. You and I know I haven't, but they don't. These guys shoot first, then worry about smoothing the mess over. They will assume you're helping me and they won't ask any questions. Understand?"

She nodded and opened her mouth, but shut it again without speaking. Her eyes were blinking furiously.

"Come on, then. We've got to go." I turned with her hand still in mine and we began walking as briskly as damp sand and our bruised bodies would allow toward scrubby trees that marked where the mainland ended and the point began. Even if the incoming tide didn't cover our tracks, we would be almost impossible to track through the rockfield. My stomach was queasy; I kept marching.

We climbed through broken rocks that shifted beneath our feet. In ten minutes we were both soaked with sweat. As we climbed, Beth tried to question me further, but I ignored her. Lies wouldn't resolve her doubts and the truth wouldn't help anybody right now. However, I couldn't ignore the twisting in my guts. I wasn't quite a murderer, at least not yet. What I really had become I was afraid to face. You get that way when you cross over the line so many times that you're not clear any longer on what's right or wrong. Drinking lubricates those crossings. I'd sold my pride and my soul for whiskey, ranking me right up there with Esau. Praying wasn't my thing, but I said a short one then. Didn't ask for much, only for forgiveness and for both of us to go on living. Didn't seem like too much to ask for.

By mid-morning we were out of the rocks and through the narrow stand of trees. Now the ground was more open, with grasslands and, here and there, a line of scraggly trees to break up the terrain. By noon we were seeing stone fences and narrow paths.

Late afternoon sun beat on our backs. Our shadows slogged ahead of us, wavering now and then before gathering themselves and marching forward.

"Damn, it's hot, Frank."

"I know."

"Do you have any idea where we're headed?"

"Sure, eastward."

"Eastward to where, to what?" Her words were punctuated by quick intakes of air. We were working our way up another grass-covered slope, one in a seemingly endless series.

"Don't know. We're bound to hit a road or a village soon. We've seen fences on and off for hours."

"Frank, that water we drank from the stream back there, I mean I know it looked clean, but how sanitary do you think it was?"

I paused for a moment in the shade of a towering rock ledge. "Fairly safe, I'd say. No livestock to foul it. Anyway, it was drink or die. Rather take my chances on bad water. Come on, we'd better keep pushing."

The ground was noticeably drier now. A puff of dust rose with each step. Oaks and pines of the coast had given way to gnarly mesquite and creosote bushes and the grass was brown and poor. "Speak any Spanish?" I asked.

"A little. Took two semesters of French at UK, but I had a Spanish class my junior year at Bourbon County and spent three weeks in Madrid one summer."

"See the Prado?"

"Yes."

"Weren't the Goyas magnificent?"

"Incredible. So dark and moving."

"See a bullfight?"

"Yes."

"Plaza de Toros?"

"Sí."

"Like it?"

Beth paused and wiped the sweat off her forehead with the back of her left forearm. Lines of sweat had run down her face smearing her remaining makeup. Impossible now to tell where art ended and reality began.

"Liked the music and the costumes and the horses prancing and the freshly raked dirt. Suppose I liked the atmosphere, the excitement. As a spectacle it was superb. But..."

"The blood."

"Yes, the blood, and death being so ritualized. And the people drank and shouted and sweated and cried out for more blood. And after everyone had stabbed the poor bull this thin, dark man in his fancy suit put in the sword. Think that's how you say it. Then, after the bull had given his life for this glorious spectacle, they simply hauled his carcass away. So inhuman, especially after he'd tried so hard."

"But he was dead."

"Yes. Still the fight seems so unequal. The bull has to fight so many, he has to die, and then they tie up his hooves and drag him out with his face in the dust."

"At least he gets to fight." We were moving again and the slope was steeper now and we had to pull ourselves from one rock to another.

"Yes, but he dies."

"So do we all."

"But not stabbed to death in front of thousands of people."

I had no answer to that, although I wondered what difference the manner of death made to a dead man. After another mile we came to a flat, gray rock and I sat down and looked back the way we had come. The ground seemed to slide away into the pool of red and gold shimmering on the western horizon. The bull was still on my mind.

"You know the bull we were talking about? True, he died. But at least the son-of-a-bitch died fighting."

"Goddamn, Frank. You act like it's a glorious death. Speaking of death, I'm dying for a drink, and I don't mean water."

"So am I, my rather bedraggled queen, so am I."

35

At first I thought they were a mirage.

Dusk was falling and I was scouring the countryside for a suitable spot to spend the night. Sharp-edged rocks scattered between low-slung bushes were all I'd found. Then, low on the southeastern horizon, I saw, or thought I saw, pinpoints of light. I blinked and squinted. A handful of lights danced a jagged Congo line.

Beth was twenty yards ahead of me, working her way down from the mesa top. I called to her.

"Look. Over to your right. Lights. May be a village."

"Where? I can't see them."

"Low on the horizon. Look to the southeast, beyond the bend of that arroyo."

"Damn, Frank. I still can't see anything. How far away?"

"A mile, maybe two. Come here and I'll show you. We need to go down from here anyway. I see a path that heads in the right direction."

I waited for her as she scrambled up ground she had already crossed. She was panting when she reached me and dust from the hillside had powdered her face. It was a fine, light brown, and her lips were parted slightly. I had a sudden urge to kiss her and I didn't wait. After a moment, neither did she.

"What was that all about?" Beth asked.

"I'm not sure. Blame Mexico." In the strangely alive dusk I could see lights dancing in her eyes. "Like it?"

A moment of silence squeezed between us. "A little," she said. "Did you?"

I nodded.

Twilight was the color of an overripe plum. The moon was cautiously eyeing us through the fissure in a rock wall that rose from the southern end of our mesa. Stars were sprinkled against the ebony sky like handfuls of confectioner's sugar flung by a temperamental god. Moonlight shimmered on the narrow path. Time to move.

Her lips were parted and her tongue played in the shadowy corners of her mouth. In the moonlight her teeth shone white. I put my right hand behind her head. Her hair was soft and ran through my fingers like water. I pulled her face to mine. Our mouths sought and found each other. Her breath was warm and sweet in my mouth.

By mutual consent we separated and began to walk single file down the path. When it widened on the valley floor her hand slid into mine as we marched toward the dancing lights.

36

Streets of dust between buildings of stone. Only lamplight spilling from open windows and a smattering of security lights haphazardly marking the way. We came into the village from the west through a wide-mouthed draw. When the rains came it would fill to overflowing with swirling brown water. Now it was full of fine brown dust that rose around our feet.

No people walked the main street as we intersected it at a sweeping bend. A yellow and brown mongrel padded by, his short tail ramrod straight in the night. If he knew we were there, he never let on. My empty stomach growled.

"Right or left?"

Beth paused, looked first left then right. Left was a small unlighted house decorated by a low rock fence running before it and an old Ford station wagon up on concrete blocks. Looking the other way, I could see dark, heavy structures lounging in shadows and long, narrow pools of lights spilling across dark ground.

"Right. There's some light. Maybe there are some people."

"And water and food."

"God, yes. I've never been as thirsty, so hungry, so tired. Frank Kohler, you sure know how to treat a girl."

"Let's hope the people here are generous."

"Why?"

"I don't have much money. Do you?"

"No, none. Oh, hell."

"What is it, Beth? Did you hurt yourself?"

"No, but I just realized I don't have my purse. I left it in the hotel room. That means not only do I not have any money, but I also don't have a smidgen of identification."

We scrambled up out of the draw and started down the dirt road. The ground was firm and level and the walking seemed easy after the rocky, uneven floor of the draw. I reached over and gave Beth a pat on the head. "That's good in a way, you know."

"How in hell do you figure that?"

"Since you have no identification, you can be whomever you want to be. Sort of like starting all over again. Not many people get a second chance in life like that."

She shrugged, looked up, and made an effort to smile. "Not sure I welcome that chance." I laughed at her, but only a little. Seemed to me to be an attractive option. But then I suppose when a man got in a mess like the one I'd stepped in almost anything else has appeal.

There was no traffic on the road. We moved from one shimmering pool of lamplight to another, passing houses full of light with men and women moving about within. I was tempted to stop, but afraid to go knocking on doors after dark in the soft evening of a strange land. We kept moving, plodding past abandoned buildings and collapsing barns. The road ran straight for a quarter of a mile, then made a sharp turn to the right where it connected with a paved road.

"More lights ahead," I said.

"Looks like too many for a house, unless it's a mansion."

"More likely a tavern or an inn. Too close to the road for a house."

"Who in the world would stay out here in this lonely place?"

"Oh, I don't know that it's so lonely," I said. "It's on a paved road that undoubtedly leads from somewhere to somewhere. People must travel between the two places. Then there might be some people who would come here simply to get away from the multitudes."

"But it's so desolate."

"Remember, Beth, you're seeing it in the dark."

"And sober."

"Yeah, we are sober."

"Disgustingly so," she said and we pushed on through the gauzy, violet evening, listening to the night birds, feeling the breeze against our hot dry skin, smelling meat and onions and peppers cooking, tasting the grit of Mexico on our tongues. After a while I felt the smoothness of Beth's palm slip into mine. I didn't say a word, just squeezed very gently and kept walking under a sky larger and darker than the ones I remembered from Kentucky.

We were just two little, lonely, insignificant figures journeying toward an unknown destination in a vast galaxy. It crossed my mind that to strangers we might have looked like sweethearts out for an evening stroll, or maybe a husband and wife. What we really were, I decided, were two strangers bound together by a benevolent God, on a pilgrimage to recover their lost souls. A mysterious notion that I could walk forever through the encompassing darkness filled my mind.

"You know what, Frank?" Beth's voice was sharp and loud. I jerked and stumbled and caught my breath.

"What?"

"We need a drink. Things always look better after you have a drink."

"Different anyway."

"No, Frank. You are unappreciative of the blessings of alcohol. Trust me on this. Things looks better after one drink, much better after two. Anyway, I could sure as hell use a stiff one right now. How about you?"

"Wouldn't say no."

We walked on through the moonlight.

37

"How much for the room?"

The man rubbed his face. Flesh jiggled like little bobbing dogs in the back of a family's sedan.

"Fifty dollars, American."

I shook my head. "Don't have that kind of money on me." I felt Beth's body sag against me. I wasn't sure how much longer she could hold up. "Like I told you, we had an accident back up the road and my traveler's checks were lost. Only cash I have is what I had in my wallet, and I have already spent much here on food and wine."

"Well," he said through fleshy lips that lurked below a bushy black mustache, "it is late and I do have the room. Twenty-five dollars, American."

"It's two o'clock in the morning and you were just going to bed. You already have your nightshirt on. If you don't rent the room to me you won't rent it tonight, and you know it. Five dollars."

"Fifteen. I must pay the maid and change the sheets and keep the records." He let his mustache droop to show how sad he was.

Beth poked me in the ribs.

"Ten. Take it or I'm gone."

The mustache twitched again. "Señor, please, stay the night of course. I will give you one of our finest rooms. If you will only sign the register."

I gave him a slightly damp, crinkled picture of Alexander Hamilton and wrote Ernest Hemingway on the line below where someone whose first name was illegible and last name was Duran had signed. Duran had signed the day before.

The fat man gave me a phony smile and an elongated, old-fashioned, metal key to number five. Unencumbered by luggage, I half carried Beth up the fourteen steps to the second floor. As we walked down the dimly lit hallway we could hear the sounds of tinkling glass from the bar below. Along the hallway, wallpaper was peeling sporadically, leaving matadors who were now only half a man fighting bulls without horns or tails.

There were only ten rooms, and we found number five at the far end of the hall. The knob turned in my hand and we stumbled inside.

Musty odors of old sweat, spent sex, and lost youth competed for prominence as I guided Beth down on the bed and flung open panels of glass.

Moonlight streamed in through the open window and caressed Beth's face. With her hands folded beneath her head she looked like a little girl. As if to counter that image, the tops of her breasts thrust up to greet the moonlight.

Beth was asleep before I even got my shoes off. For some time I sat in my underwear in a cracked leather chair and watched moon- light move across her sleeping face. When the moon had temporarily hidden itself behind the branches of the cottonwood tree outside the window, I crossed the dusty wooden floor and eased down beside her. I kissed her bare shoulders and her cheeks and her eyelids. Then I turned onto my back and stared at the water-stained ceiling until there was only silence and darkness.

38

I awoke with a face full of sunlight. From the quality of the light I could tell that it was well after daylight, but not high noon. Birds were noisy in the trees and a breeze ruffled the faded curtains.

Leaving Beth sleeping, I dressed and went downstairs. Yellowed wallpaper and rotting carpet looked more shabby in the morning light than it had the night before. However, there was a wonderful curve to the dark wood of the banister I hadn't noticed and the bones of the old inn were good.

A new, younger man was behind the check-in counter. He had on a clean, white shirt and his black hair was slicked back. It glistened beneath the overhead lights.

"*Buenos dios*, señor."

"Good morning."

"A cup of coffee, perhaps?"

"Yes, please."

"*Lache.*"

"No, *negro*."

He smiled, and poured into twin china cups from a large metal carafe. He poured with style. The cups had roses painted on the sides.

"You pour well."

"*De nada.* How can I assist you, Señor Hemingway?"

I sipped at the coffee, managing to scald my tongue, but returned his smile anyway. "My wife and I have had an accident and are without transportation. Can you help us?"

"*Sí.* You can rent a car." He named a large town, and a price I couldn't afford.

"Thank you, but when we had our accident we lost our luggage. Our traveler's checks were in the suitcase. So..." I shrugged my shoulders.

"A bus?"

"Something private, yet inexpensive?"

"There is a man who has a small truck. He lives just beyond the edge of town. For a price he might drive you. Where are you going?"

"Our plans are unclear at this point. Can you get word to him this morning?"

The man sipped at his coffee and studied me across the top of the cup. "Sí. I can send my son, on his bicycle. Luis will be home from school at noon. Can you wait?"

"Yes, I can wait, but tell your son to hurry."

"You are in big hurry, no?"

"Naturally my wife and I want to see all of Mexico we can. This is our vacation. We only have a few days left."

He nodded and stared at the dark liquid in his cup. When he raised his eyes he found my face. "I understand. I will have my wife go to school. It is less than a mile from here. Luis will not mind. Always he favors the sunshine over the science. Please excuse me."

I watched him quick-step across the room and exit through an opening, half-hidden in shadows. He walked with a stiff back and measured step and I wondered if he had once been a soldier, or a policeman. I stayed at the counter and sipped my coffee. The air was warmer now and I could no longer hear the birds.

When I returned to room number five Beth was sitting up in bed bathed in sunlight.

"Where have you been?"

"Making arrangements."

"What kind?"

"To get us the hell out of Dodge, my darling."

She turned her face up to mine. "Frank?"

"Yes."

"Can I ask you a question?"

"Sure."

She worked her head to one side. "I was wondering why we don't just go ahead and call Preston? He has to have heard by now and he might be worried sick. One long distance call can't cost too much. If you don't have a phone card or cash we can make it collect."

My stomach felt queasy. I sat down on a corner of the bed. "Beth, we need to talk."

"Frank, we are."

"No, we're not. At least not the sort of talk I mean."

Beth was suddenly very still. Her face was angled so that it was half in sunlight, half in shade. Flesh not touched by sunlight looked frozen. I wanted a drink as badly as I'd ever wanted one. My voice broke as I said her name.

"What?"

The room suddenly seemed unbearably hot. Pushing myself off my corner of the bed, I walked across the room and stood with my back to her, looking out the window.

Below the sunlit courtyard was sprinkled with smooth, white stones. An old brown dog was lying very still under ancient trees with black twisted limbs and leaves so thick they shut out the sun. I turned to face her. My shirt was damp with sweat. Inside my mind the plates shifted.

"I don't know how to say this, Beth."

"Is it that bad?"

"Worse."

"About me?"

"Yes."

"Well," she said, eyes moving to find my face. "Say it, and tell it straight. Lying is no good. I've lied all my life, and I've been lied to for as long as I can remember. It's no damn good this lying. Lying only leads to more lying, and ultimately the only way out from under the mountain of lies is through the bottle."

I couldn't face her, not with what I had to say. Not then. So I turned until I was again looking at the hot dry courtyard. For a long time I couldn't think of how to say it. Finally words came and I spoke. "You know, it's funny, but you are right about the lies and the bottle. We both tell lies. We both drink too much."

I waited for her to speak. All I could hear was the faint twitter of birds and now and then a muffled noise from the floor below. Then the birds fell silent and I turned around. She was lying flat on her back, arms by her sides, staring straight up at the ceiling. Both of her eyes were open wide. She looked at me, then turned away.

"We don't drink the same though, Frank."

"How do you mean that, Beth?"

"You drink to forget, while I drink to remember."

"Remember what?"

"The good times. The times when I was young and beautiful and happy. When people, really nice people, truly loved me. When I wanted to live."

I went over and perched on the edge of the bed. I felt like an uncertain vulture.

"Living is what we need to talk about."

"Why, Frank? Why should we talk about our problems? Talking about them doesn't help. It only helps make them real."

My thoughts tumbled over each other until I shut my mind down and started talking. I didn't know how to say what I had to say in a soft way, so I just said it. "Press doesn't want you to live, Beth."

"I know." Her voice was very soft, fading like it was falling in on itself.

"What do you mean, you know?"

"I know he doesn't want me in his life in any way."

"I'm not talking about divorce here."

"I know, Frank." She turned her face and looked at me as if I were a little child. "We are talking about the other d word."

"The other d word?"

"Death. I know he wants me dead. Dead and out of his way so he can get on with his life and his career. I'm a weight around his neck, a hindrance, his personal handicap. Don't look so shocked, dear boy. The great man has told me so." She smiled. Smiled the way a person smiles when they see some sad event unfolding, yet know they cannot change the outcome.

"Point blank. To my face. In my face. He wants me dead and buried and gone forever."

"But, why?"

"Don't ever ask why, Frank. Asking why only makes people lie. If you can't figure why out for yourself you are too stupid to understand, even if they told you." She paused and smiled, a faint, half-erased smile that made you wonder what she was really thinking.

"This time I'll tell you, Frank. You really are innocent. Innocent and ignorant of evil. You think you are all macho, still Joe College Hero on a golden autumn Saturday afternoon."

I started to say the words that filled my throat. Instead, I swallowed them.

"Well, it's later than you think and you don't know a damn thing about the real world. You are just a big, sweet, good-looking, dumb guy, still running interference for a man who can't carry your jock strap. You're hiding behind a pair of moldy shoulder pads and a bottle.

Wake up, Frank. Wake up before it is too late. Preston gave up on me when I turned thirty, got a tummy, and began to face reality. He thinks he is so goddamn perfect that everybody around him has to be perfect, too. Only not quite as perfect as he is. No, that would never do. He lives for the praises of men with thick wallets who can't make three foot putts and anorexic blondes who give him blow jobs between luncheons and tell him what a stud he is."

I started to say something, anything to stop the torrent of words, but she put a finger across my lips.

"Don't say anything, Frank. You'd only waste your breath. I embarrass him when I drink, and when I forget to cook supper, or can't remember the name of his latest deep pocket supporter, or when I forget to come home at night.

So I drink, so what? I drink to remember before Preston Big Stud Marshall, when I was a real person and I had true friends and my mom and dad loved me. Well, my friends have forgotten me and mom and dad are both dead and I think I'll join them. Only my way. See, Frank, my goal is to drink myself to death. And I am very good at achieving goals. You know I had a goal to be a cheerleader at UK, and I made it. I had a goal to marry Preston Marshall, and I made it. Now my goal is to drink myself to death, and I'll make it."

"Don't be stupid, Beth."

"I'm not stupid, Frank. Don't you be. I'm very smart. I've quit believing all the goddamn lies. The only truths are in the bottle, and death, and I'll make it yet."

"Don't talk that way." I could feel anger bubbling inside me. I was very angry.

"Why not? Drinking is a little expensive, but it is slow and soft and sweet. What's wrong with a girl wanting slow and soft and sweet?"

"Life can be good again."

"No, it can't. Not for me. For a few hours back there I thought it might be with you, but I know now that it's too late. We'll never make it, not the way real people should."

"I don't see why not, Beth?"

"Because, you big, dumb fullback, I don't want it now, not the way you and I are. Not the way we drink and the way I'm going to go on drinking. Oh, if I'd fallen in love with you all those years ago, or, to be totally truthful, admitted that love and swallowed my ego it might all have been different.

But, oh no, I convinced myself that I was in love with an All-American, and maybe I was, in a way I never have quite been able to define. Anyway, I lived to marry him when I should have been listening to my heart. But Frank, the heart is fragile and needs protecting while the ego is the strongest thing going. And I was weak and took the wrong path." She smiled. "A wrong path through a dark, pestilent wood, and here we are."

She lifted her head and kissed me, very lightly, on the lips. Then she fell back and turned away from me. I sat beside her and rubbed her soft back. The light in the room slowly changed and the birds began to sing again in the trees. Before dark the man with the moveable mustache came up and told us our transportation was ready.

Beth got up and washed her face. Then she put her arm through mine and we walked down the once elegant stairs together, leaning against each other in a casual way, like a long-married couple. In a way we were married, only to the bottle.

We walked through the lobby and into the courtyard. The sun had fallen behind the hills and under the dark trees the air was hot and still and close. I helped her into the truck. Her legs were trembling and my hands had started to shake.

She sat between me and the driver. He was a small, very brown man who smoked black cigarettes and hummed. He told me his name was Domingo. I gave him the money and told him my name was Ernest Hemingway and Beth's was Hadley. Beth smiled, but said nothing.

Domingo asked me where I wanted him to drive. I looked out the window, sweating a little, and considered my options. None appeared promising. Beth's words about the lies men tell kept haunting me, so I told him the truth, at least all of it he needed to know. I told him we'd lost our money and I needed work to pay our way back across the border.

He studied my face for a minute, then said he had a cousin who could get me work in the vegetable fields. I nodded and we started rolling.

It was very hot in the truck. Beth looked straight ahead. No one spoke. I needed a drink. Beth's hands were shaking harder and she looked down at them, then closed her eyes.

I rolled down the window and looked at flat, brown fields full of low-growing grain. Uneven rows of dark trees lined the fields and in the distance the mountains were hard and black.

Warm air rushed into the truck and dust from the road covered my face. I sat with Beth soft and warm against me and looked out the window at the dying day until it was too dark to see. Then for a long time I thought about Preston and Lethridge and the demons that danced at the bottom of bottles and how I could no longer slow dance with whiskey. The price was simply too great. I'd fallen off the ledge, only to find my fall broken by another ledge. I couldn't stand another fall. Somewhere in the sweat-scented Mexican night I drifted off to sleep. My last conscious thought was that the taste of Beth's kiss was still on my lips.

39

The rows were straight and long and in the faraway fields that kissed the sides of the mountains grain billowed before the morning breeze. Cattle, sleek and black, grazed in the pastures south of the houses. Day after day white clouds plastered themselves against a hard blue sky.

Six days a week I rose before dawn to work in the fields. Muscles I hadn't used in years ached in protest each morning as I ate a piece of fruit, chewed on crusty bread, and drank a cup of coffee before I caught a ride in the back of an aging red truck. Every morning before I left I kissed Beth softly as she slept. As I kissed her soft lips I smelled the whiskey on her breath and the urgings rose in me. I turned my face, but it was hard. Oh God, was it hard.

We worked corn, peppers, tomatoes, and fourteen varieties of melons. Most days I worked with two experienced hands, Juan and Rueben. Just after daylight, the truck would drop us off. As darkness fell it would pick us up.

We'd been picking tomatoes for a week. Each day burned hotter than the one before. Sunlight charred my skin to bronze and sucked the juice from my flesh.

"Sure is hot today, no, Señor Joe?"

"Yeah," I said. I was going by Joe now. Changing names was easy. Changing anything else important seemed impossible. "Does it ever cool down?" I asked Juan.

"Sí. When the fall comes, it will get cooler. Some winters there will even be snow on the top of the blue mountain."

"It is not so hot where you come from?" Rueben was a younger man, short, and slim-hipped. Sweat glistened in his black hair.

"Hot, and more humid, but not hot like this."

"Do you like it here?" asked Rueben. Being younger, he was less restrained in his questioning.

"Seems like a nice place." Already I could feel the strain on my back from bending over. It was only mid-morning.

"Better than the United States?"

"Rueben, you ask too many questions." Juan spoke with the authority of a village elder, or a familiar uncle.

I wiped sweat out of my eyes with one of the soft white rags the farm provided. "That's okay. Makes the day go faster. In some ways I like it better. Other ways, not so well." I stood up straight for a moment. Muscles in my lower back burned.

"Guess, all things considered, this is the best spot for me to be right now," I said. My chosen name sounded good to me, too. Anonymity surrounded the word like a familiar old quilt.

"You sound like Juan," Rueben said. "He is always telling the young men to stop and smell the coffee. Of course, he means enjoy what they have and ask for nothing more."

"Savor the moment."

"Sí."

"As usual, Rueben, you hear the words, but do not truly listen." Juan put down his basket and mopped at his face. "I do not say to never strive for better, only to live each day to its fullest, and not spend it with idle dreams and worries of problems that may never exist and complaints about things over which you have no control."

"Listen to who is talking. Old man, when you were younger did you not leave the village and seek your fame and fortune in Mexico City?" Rueben continued to pick as he spoke. Deep in his eyes there were lights I couldn't fathom.

"There, and elsewhere. I traveled much, and saw much, and learned much when I was a young man."

"Tell us again, oh great Juan, of your exploits on the silver screen and in the squared circle."

"You have heard it all before, Rueben. Didn't your family teach you to respect your elders, not to make fun of them?"

"But you are my father figure of the fields. I must look to you for hope and inspiration while the sun is in the sky. If not, I would have to resign myself to a life of picking vegetables, and that I could not stand. If life was only tomatoes and corn and beans I would kill myself. But, that is too tragic a thought for such a beautiful day, and our new amigo, Joe, he has not heard of the exploits of Juan Ordenz, star of the silver screen, prize fighter most excellent, and tomato picker without equal."

"Enough, Rueben. Sí, I was an actor in a few movies, many years ago when I was young and had my full head of hair. I was even, what do you call it, *banana dos*, a few times, but not pretty enough to be the big star. Also, the directors said I lacked a certain emotion."

"But you were a champion boxer."

"Of Mexico only. Do not go making me that which I am not. I am quite capable of doing that myself."

"What weight?" I asked.

"Middleweight."

Rueben leaned forward from his row. "Do not denigrate yourself, old man. Be full of pride. You fought for the world championship."

"Not really, my son. Only for the championship of the western hemisphere sponsored by some boxing group that existed for only a few years. The World Circuit of Boxing, or some such." He shrugged and smiled. "Too long ago to remember details."

"Who did you fight?" I asked. "I used to follow boxing."

"This was well before your time, amigo. I am an old man." Juan smiled. I wondered what he was remembering.

"After I decisioned Gomez in fifteen, in Tijuana in August, I fought a Canadian, named Pffeifer, on the first day of November. He was shorter than me, and I pounded on the top of his head all evening. His head was very hard, however, like granite, and I did no serious harm.

We fought indoors in Toronto on a platform above a hockey rink. He was a good body puncher. Had a wicked left hand. But he could not hurt my body. In those days I was stone.

It was a good fight. Fifteen rounds. Everyone got their money's worth. Pffeifer was a Canadian. So the decision was easy for the judges. They sent the crowd home happy and me back to Mexico. In another year or two the legs began to go. Always the legs go first. When I could no longer dance with the young lions, I quit and came home."

"And lived happily ever after."

"Do not make fun of others, Rueben. Your words will come back to haunt you. But yes, I am happy. I saved some of the money I made, and all of the memories. Money is convenient, but the memories are what make life beautiful."

Juan stood and looked at the blue mountain. In the tomato field the air did not stir. The sunlight was hot. Sweat trickled slowly down my face. Juan's face was that of a statue. I wondered what memory he was replaying in his mind. Finally he shrugged and picked up his basket. "Come, amigos. Time again to pick tomatoes."

That evening the truck was late. We stood in the gathering dusk until we were three dark blurs in the purpling mist.

Rueben walked away until all I could see was the red glow of his cigarette. The moon seemed slow to rise and there was only darkness, and within the darkness the sounds of insects rustling in the leaves of the plants, and twice the sharp cry of a nocturnal bird.

Rueben called out from beyond his cigarette. "The truck is very late tonight, Juan."

"Sí."

"It may have broken down."

"It has before."

"Sí. Did you hear that strange pinging sound this morning?"

"Sí. I also smelled a bad odor. Like a rotten tomato."

"You have been in the fields too long, old man."

"That is probably true. Yet I plan to keep on working in these fields."

"For the rest of your life?"

"With the grace of God."

"Since when did you become a religious man?" Rueben asked.

"All men are religious in one form or another, at one time or another."

"When they are boys, perhaps."

"No, Rueben, all men are always boys in their hearts, but they all become very close to God when they grow older. Some are close all their lives, others for brief periods that come and go like the clouds, still others only in the final moments before death."

Rueben came walking toward us. I followed his advance by the glow of his cigarette. Juan was so close that I could stretch out my arm and touch him, yet his body was more shadow than substance.

Rueben was close now, his voice loud in the silent sundown. "You are taking the easy way out, old man. Every man has to die. It is only a matter of time."

Juan chuckled. "Then it is only a matter of time before he gets religion. Ask the thief on the cross."

I could smell cigarette smoke on Rueben's breath and hear anger trembling in his voice. "I tell you this, Señor Juan who knows so much, before you can die you have to truly live. For if you do not live, how can you die? I tell you most people don't really live. They don't really drink from the cup of life. They are content with Coca-Cola, beer, or liquor instead of lifting life to their lips. I can feel it. I am wasting away in these godforsaken fields."

"God has not forsaken these fields."

"I don't see him down here picking tomatoes under the boiling hot sun, old man."

"Perhaps he has been here. Perhaps he is here among us this evening as a stranger."

"Juan, please. Do not make me laugh. The gringo is not God or his son or even a saint. Joe College is just another tomato picker in hell."

Juan stirred beside me. "He can leave. You can leave. Freedom is there for any who needs it badly enough. Just be sure leaving is what you want to do. Great valleys are often very dark at the bottom. Make sure you have the courage, the will."

"Do you doubt my courage?" Rueben asked.

"It does not matter whether or not I, or Joe, or any man doubts it. What matters is when the moment of majesty comes you have it."

Juan leaned toward me and clapped me on the shoulder. "Come, amigo. We must go. The old truck must have broken down. It will not come for us tonight, and our beans and tequila and women await us."

He stepped into the darkness and was gone. I followed the sounds of his leaving. In five minutes we had crossed the broken ground and were on the firm, flat road. I could smell the dirt stirred by our feet. The moon had finally begun to rise. It hung mashed between crags of the blue mountain like a pale overripe orange. Pinpoints of starlight began to pop through the dark ceiling of the night. Before we had traveled a mile on the road I could smell cigarette smoke behind me.

40

Rueben whistled. Not his usual low morbid drone, today he was sharp and shrill, the notes dancing on the light breeze. We were finishing the late corn now, searching the rows to capture what the machines had missed. Juan and I were side by side in separate rows. Rueben was twenty yards ahead, one row to Juan's right. Stalks were thick and dry, and they rustled in hushed tones as we brushed against them.

"The boy is happy today, Juan. Any idea why?"

Juan turned and looked at me and smiled, his hands still busy in the corn. "Tomorrow we do not work."

"Why won't we be working on Thursday?"

"Ah, I remember now. This is your first season. Tomorrow is the start of the Fiesta. It will run for three days and three nights. Then, on Sunday, there will be rest. Some will go to Mass, of course, but those who need it most will just rest. On Monday we will work again."

"I've heard about other fiestas. What's the purpose for this one? To honor a saint? Or to provide an opportunity to get drunk?"

"Ah, Joe, you doubt the sincerity of my people. The fiesta is to celebrate the harvest." Juan's hands moved among the rustling corn leaves, and he laughed. "But you are closer to the truth than it makes me comfortable to admit. Many will drink, some will get drunk, a few will get very drunk. But not all. Even at Fiesta there are those who prefer to judge others rather than enjoying life."

He smiled at me, a gap-toothed smile. What teeth he had were crooked and yellow. "You, of course, will come, amigo. You and your señora."

I wanted to tell someone the truth. It's an absolute suffering to know the truth and want to tell it and yet not be able to tell it. Because once you tell the truth there is no putting it back in the bottle. I liked Juan too well to lie to him, but didn't know him well enough to tell the particular truth that was hammering at my skull. So I told him a different truth.

"I'll have to check with Linda. She hasn't been feeling well."

"I had wondered. My wife said no one in the village had seen her for several days."

"She's had a virus. She should be better soon."

Juan bobbed his head. It bumped against the stalks, rattling them. "She must come to Fiesta. It will do her good. Fiesta is good for everyone."

I made my hands busy in the corn. "We'll see."

The breeze had strengthened as we talked and it was whispering its way through the rows. Clouds shunted across a high sky and shadows played hide and seek in the cornfield below. Reuben's staccato whistling defined the pattern of the morning. I let its rhythm work in my brain until there was only corn, and wind, and shadows.

41

"We could go, you know," I said.

It was so dark in the room that I couldn't see my hand. Slivers of light came in only at the separation of the heavy dark curtains and at the bottom of the door. I could hear Beth's breathing.

"That's true. I suppose we could," Beth said. She was still beside me. Only her lips moved when she spoke. "But why go? We could have just as much fun by ourselves. You could bring in a bottle of tequila and we could drink until it was gone, or we were wasted." She rolled onto her side. Her face was close to mine. Alcohol was thick on her breath. "Here, have a drink." The bottle was cool against my bare chest.

"No, thanks. Last time I overdid it. Vomited blood and my stomach hurt for a week."

"You used to be a fun person, Frank. What happened to you? What happened to us?"

"Nothing has happened to me. Just can't drink like I used to."

Puking up his own blood tends to put a holy fear in a man, and strengthen his resolve. It also makes him ask profound questions like whether he wanted to live or die. Between the long days in the fields and the quiet nights, I had the luxury of time to think.

Beth snorted. "Can't or won't?"

"Bit of both."

"It's can't. You men are all alike. You and Preston, two bastard blood-brothers under the skin. You can drink all you want to, but if a girl has a few drinks it offends your delicate male sensibilities. Then, all of a sudden, you are just too goody-goody to have a drink with a girl."

"We can have a drink together at the fiesta tomorrow."

"Promises, promises. Just like all the other men in my sordid life. You say you will, but, when it gets right down to the bone, you won't."

"I'll have a drink at Fiesta tomorrow. Maybe two. I promise. But no more. Sorry, but I can't handle liquor anymore."

The bottle shifted against my chest as Beth moved. "That's the whole point, isn't it? To lose control. Then you don't have to face reality."

"Is the bottle really better than reality, Beth?"

"The bottle demands less."

"More," I said.

Beth pushed herself up onto one elbow. Tequila gurgled in the dark.

"Don't you think you have had enough for one night?"

"You think I have a liquor problem?"

"I know I have a liquor problem. Don't know about you. Maybe. Probably. Anyway, that's one you'll have to answer for yourself."

"You think I'm a drunk?"

"I didn't say that, Beth. You'll have to decide that. What do you say we call it a night, get some sleep."

Beth rolled away from me. In the wake of her movements quiet absorbed the room. Then I heard the liquid gurgle again. Seconds later there was a smash of glass against the wall.

"Fuck you, Frank Kohler."

I wanted to say healing words, but couldn't think of any. Gradually the moon pressed its face against the window. A faint silver glimmer filled the room. I turned on my side, facing Beth. Her face was white and closed. I lay unmoving beside her.

Time seemed a lost dimension. Night surrounded us, dark and heavy and warm. I could feel its arms around me and its hot, stale breath on my face. Deep in the night, I felt the saggy mattress begin to quiver. Later, I could hear Beth's sobs.

I wanted to reach out to her. I wanted to touch her. It hurt me not to put my arms around her, but I couldn't will myself to do it. After a long time the sobs stopped.

"Kiss me, Frank."

"What?"

"You don't have to mean it, just kiss me. Please. You son-of-a-bitch, it's the least you could do. You brought me down here to kill me, but you couldn't do it. You're no more a man than Preston. Since you can't kill me, you have to kiss me. That is your sentence."

"Are you the jury or the judge?"

"The victim. The fucking victim. Frank, I'm starting to sober up, so kiss me before I puke my guts out."

I found her face with my hands and mashed my lips against hers. They were soft and full and wet. Tequila was on her breath and tears dampened her cheeks. She slid her arms around my neck and pulled me to her until my neck ached. Her hands became busy below my waist. When I entered her, she was soft and warm and wet. She moaned just once, very softly.

The sound was almost an apology, or a confession.

Reverberations in the dark woke me. Night still held the room and the wind was up. I could hear it gnawing at the wooden door. I could also hear Beth crying. Her head was buried in her pillow and her back was to me. I ran my hands across the smooth ivory flesh until dawn came. Then I kissed the back of her neck and got up and dressed and stepped outside without speaking.

42

Candles flickered in every window. At the end of Hidalgo Street a bonfire burned. Flames licked at the soft, dark underbelly of the night sky. They were orange and, deep in the middle, electric blue.

We were walking down Hidalgo toward the fire. Beth was sipping wine from a small green bottle encased in straw. The straw was brown and woven together into a basket shaped like an oriole's nest. She was just starting on her second bottle.

I'd drunk a Mexican beer after lunch, and another after supper. Figured I could handle beer, but by dusk my stomach had started to hurt. Simply to ease the pain I drank two swallows of tequila. Just now I'd finished off the last of the first bottle of wine. The tequila had tasted good, the wine too sweet. A small hammer was starting to pound rhythmically against the back wall of my brain.

A side street, poorly lighted, ran into Hidalgo from the west. A grocery store stood on that corner atop a natural rise. An elevated porch ran the width of the store and a fistful of men leaned against the wooden rail that fronted the porch. Juan was at the end of the line nearest us.

"Come on, there's Juan. You've heard me talk about him. Let's go over and say hello."

"I don't want to." Beth's voice sounded shrill. I blamed the shrillness on the wine and the night air.

I took her hand in mine and gave it a tug. As we crossed the street she drank from the bottle. The wind was kicking up again and dust danced before us.

"Hey, Juan."

He turned and smiled. Lines in his face ran like the cracked ground of a drying riverbed. "Amigo."

"Like you to meet my lady, Linda."

Juan bowed and shook her hand with great gravity. "Linda, that is a very beautiful name. It fits you well."

"Hello. Would you like some wine?"

He eyed the bottle in the basket. "No, thank you. I have promised myself some tequila later." He turned his head. "Joe, are you not celebrating?"

"Oh, yes. Too much already. Beer and tequila and just now some wine."

"Mixing your drinks can be dangerous, amigo."

"I'm a fairly dangerous hombre." I was feeling the lift now. Everything seemed extraordinarily clear and fine.

In the faint light from the bonfire and the candles it was difficult to read Juan's expression. His face looked like leather. Skin was drawn fine and tight across his cheekbones. His eyes were black and bottomless.

"Joe, you may be right. I have often wondered about you. Where you came from. Where you are going."

"I came here to spend fiesta with you, blown here by the wild western winds. When they are strong enough they will blow me out of here."

"To where?"

"Wherever they blow. To the next village, to the river, to the blue mountains. You know, Juan, life is a game of chance." I could hear the gurgle of the wine bottle beside me. Now I wanted a drink badly.

"The wind is kicking up. We may get a storm before the night is over. Perhaps, amigo, you will be blown out of town sooner than you think." He laughed. I laughed with him to keep him company, and to stave off the craving for the wine.

Juan stopped laughing. "Maybe we should not poke the fun," he said.

"Better to laugh than cry," I said.

"Life can be a serious matter."

"Only if you let it." I turned and took Beth carefully by one elbow. The other cradled the wine bottle. "Come on, Linda. Let's go see what else we can find at Fiesta. Juan, see you in the fields."

"Later, amigo. Nice to meet you, señora."

"Likewise," Beth said.

She was unsteady on her feet and I helped her cross the street. We took small, short steps like two old people. She kept a firm grip on the wine bottle.

"Behind the school they are roasting a pig," Juan called after us. He spoke other words, but the rising wind pulled the clarity from them and I heard only sound. I raised an arm and waved.

We crossed the street without looking back. Dust was swirling and getting in everywhere. When we had crossed Hidalgo and rounded the corner, I took the wine from Beth and washed the dust out of my throat. The bottle was nearly empty. Holding hands, we walked down the narrow street. We were looking for booze. Candles flickered in the windows and wind whispered in our ears.

The shop was in a blind alley. The proprietor was middle-aged, with a face full of old acne scars. His droopy mustache matched the color of his mud brown eyes. He sold beer in small amber bottles, three brands of tequila, and wine.

I'd been so good for so long that when I was bad again I felt exceptionally fine. I'd sworn I'd never drink again, and now... Guess old habits die hard. Or is it fools never learn?

We chose a bottle of cheap red and the smallest bottle of tequila. I carried them to the counter and placed them on the polished wood. Beneath my feet the floorboards felt uneven and all four walls had a sway-backed look.

I dug a handful of coins out and offered them to the man. He took a little over half, counting them carefully, and putting them away one at a time into a wooden box with several slots.

I picked up both bottles and gave the wine to Beth. "*Gracias*," I said.

"*De nada.*"

He walked us to the door, studying our faces. As the dark swallowed us up, I said to Beth, "He won't forget us."

Drinking had resurrected ghosts in my mind. They answered to the names Press and Lethridge. I felt a sudden urge to look for Lethridge in the shadows. Apparently, the past was always just one drink away. I told myself I had to quit. But then I had told myself a lot of things over the years.

"Why should he care about us?" Beth was working with the wine bottle, trying to get the cork out. I put the tequila bottle in my pocket and took the wine bottle from her. I could hear the rising pitch of the wind as it worked its way between buildings and down the alley. Using my teeth, I finally got the cork out. All the work made me thirsty and I took a drink. Wiping the top of the bottle with my sleeve, I handed it back to Beth.

"No reason. He just seemed awfully interested."

Beth stood in a pool of flickering candlelight that fell from the building behind us. Except for a lone candle in a window it was totally dark. "When you were picking out the wine he was staring at us."

She tipped the bottle and I watched her soft throat work. "He gave me the creeps." The drink had been a long one, and it had hit her hard. I could hear changes in her voice.

"Don't think about it. He's a fat, ugly man who probably gets few customers, even at Fiesta. Dust was thick on his shelves. Besides, we're strangers to him."

Beth took another drink. "You've been to town before." It was difficult to hear her over the wind.

"Not to his shop and not with you. American women are a rare breed down here."

"How would he know I was American?"

"I spoke and you were with me. He would know."

Beth took another drink. As we walked through the darkness the wind hammered at us from between adobe walls. Ghosts danced across my mind. I worked the tequila out of my pocket and got the cap off. Then I took a good hit. Ghosts were difficult to discourage.

No candles in the windows anymore, and then there were no windows. The building on the right was an abandoned factory, the one on the left smelled like a barn.

Chris Helvey

Beth tugged at my arm and we veered left. We worked our way down the adobe until we found the rough timbers of the door. I pushed and it swung open. The room was very dark and smelled of horses and mud and old straw.

After a couple of false starts we found a pile of hay bales. By the odor, it was last year's hay. Some of the bales had come apart and we lay down on the loose straw. Our fingers were busy with buttons and bottles. Beth began to giggle and kept it up until she was out of control. Her skin was soft and warm and moved with her laughter. I could hear thunder now, loud and close. Strange light flashed through the cracks in the adobe. The smell of horseflesh was strong.

I tried to kiss her mouth but she was laughing. Her breath smelled of wine. Her breasts tasted sweet and clean. I pulled her to me and we burrowed deeper into the hay. Beth's giggles became interspersed with moans and her cheeks were suddenly wet.

43

I reached out for her, but there was only a depression in the straw where she had lain. Her dress was dark against the straw.

I called her name. My voice echoed among the rafters. Except for me, the old barn was as empty as the tomb on the third day. My heart was beating very fast and I had trouble catching my breath. I pushed up from the straw encrusted floor and hurried outside, pulling on clothes as I went.

At the door my head started to spin and nausea engulfed me. When I finished puking I was on my knees. Blood swirled through my vomit. My whole body was shaking. Easy enough to see I was out of drinking options.

Morning air was sweet and clean and cool. Every adobe wall was freshly scrubbed by the rain that had begun and ended with the night. Wind danced lightly across a phalanx of puddles. A brown dog rounded the corner at a trot, his tail curled tightly against his hindquarters.

The street lay open before me, damp and empty beneath bright morning light. Wind and rain had obliterated all traces of the passage of the night. I chose left because it led out of town, and put one foot before the other. My legs were weak and my stomach queasy. I kept walking.

I walked until all the houses lay a mile or more behind me. I called her name until my throat ached, but only the wind answered. I turned and retraced my steps, but saw no more than I'd seen before. My head ached and my stomach churned. Sunlight burned my face and my vision was blurred. I wondered if I was going blind. A hangover tortures a man's mind.

Just before dark I found her. She was lying in a shallow irrigation ditch on the northwest side of town. Blood trickled from both her nostrils and vomit was splattered across her face and thick in her hair.

She clutched an empty wine bottle in her left hand. Her right hand held a fistful of dirt. She was naked. Tears filled my eyes. I was so weak and tired.

By midnight I had her home. All the way it had been step, step, put her down, sit down and rest. Then struggle up again, pick her up, step, step, put her down, sit down and rest. The last hour had been pure agony.

The door had no lock. I pushed it open with my foot and stumbled across the room. Beth was heavy and still as a log. Her mouth hung open and she snored gently.

We fell together across the bed. For some time I lay with her in my arms. Earlier, I'd pulled off my shirt and slipped her arms through the sleeves so now I was naked above the waist and she was naked below.

I lay still and let strength ebb back into my body. When I was able, I slid out from beneath her heavy, limp body and forced myself to stand. I found the dishpan, then wandered through the deserted square to the well where I drew a bucket of water and filled the pan. Then, taking great care with each step, I walked back to our shack.

Using a piece of soft, old toweling, I washed her face and body. Her forehead and cheeks felt warm. By the time I finished my hands were trembling and the water in the pan was dark.

I covered Beth's softly rounded body with our best blanket, put the pan on the oak table, and sat down in our only chair. Pinpoints of light danced before my eyes. I closed my eyes and waited for the demons. A sensation that nothing would ever be quite the same again flowed through my mind. I was in a sardonic, melancholy mood. I knew I could never drink again. I wanted a drink anyway. Night rustled around the shack and I was afraid.

44

It began, within twenty-four hours, as a cough. Within forty-eight hours, I could hear congestion deep in her chest. On the third day the fever came. I borrowed seven aspirin from a neighbor woman with a generous heart and dark hair above her upper lip. When the fever persisted, I rolled out before dawn and walked three miles to Taluchaupa where there was a doctor. After waiting an hour and a half I finally got to explain Beth's condition.

The doctor wore a gray pin-striped suit too snug in the waist and going thin in the elbows. His plump face competed with his black doctor's bag to see which could hold more cracks and grooves. His eyes were olive brown and his hair was a series of sculptured silver waves. After listening politely, he excused himself and went into his receptionist's area, pulling the door to behind him with a click.

I could half-hear muted Spanish followed by an extended period of silence. The door opened and the doctor came back in and picked up his bag from among the papers and files that blanketed the top of his desk. He motioned for me to come along. I followed him outside onto the sun-scalded street.

His car was an ancient Buick, sporting tailfins, and painted the color of an overripe Damson plum. Rust spots the size of unrolled tortillas pitted the sides and the sunlight reflecting off the chrome was blinding. The heavy passenger side door screeched as I pulled it open. Though it had been standing with all four windows down, the interior felt like the inside of a baking oven. When he turned the small key the motor groaned, but he pumped the gas pedal and under the hood the engine roared.

I leaned back against soft upholstery, worn thin by time and sun and use. My legs were tired and it felt good to be rolling down the hard, flat roadbed with warm air blowing across my face.

"I like your car, Doctor Ramirez."

"*Gracias.*"

"What model is it?"

He turned his head away from the road for a moment and smiled at me. "It is a nineteen fifty-eight Buick Roadmaster. I got it from a young Marine in Dallas when I was doing my residency."

"How many miles does it have on it?"

He laughed, a short bark. "I don't know, señor. Not long after I purchased it I left it out in the sun all day with all the windows rolled up. Warped the speedometer and odometer. Now I can't tell how fast I am going or how far I have gone. So I live by the travels of the sun. Makes for a more, how do you say it, mellow existence." He laughed his strange, truncated laugh again.

Closing my eyes, I let the wind mash against my face. "That begs the question, doctor, what do you do when it's cloudy, or at night?"

"The lights haven't worked since last Easter, so at night I stay home, or walk, or ride a horse. When it is cloudy I use the calculated, educated estimate."

"You guess."

He laughed once again. Wind blew across my face, full of the smells of the land. Scents of dirt, and manure, and fertilizer, cows, horses, white blossoms on stunted trees all were there.

The doctor glanced at me and then back at the road. "Have you lived here long?"

"No, only a few months. Before I lived, well, let's just say on the far side of the border."

He nodded. "Forgive me for asking, but why did you come? Visitors are rare here. People from the United States almost never. Certainly not to stay."

I stared out the window and thought about his question. I thought about telling him I was trying to leave my past behind, but that seemed to lead only to more questions. I decided on a different truth. "Guess you could say I was searching for something."

The doctor twisted the wheel and we swerved around a carcass in the road. It might have been a dog, or a coyote. He grunted and a thin smile creased his face. "Guess we are all searching for something, and everybody must be somewhere. I suppose here is as good a place as any. This part of Mexico sees more than its share of strangers. Some only pass through, others stay for a time only to leave. Still others come and never leave. Have you made your decision?"

I started to answer, but then I realized I wasn't sure what my answer was. Before I could decide the road turned rough, full of ruts and uneven mounds of earth, and the doctor hit the brakes. The old car rattled through the rough places until I thought it was going to shake apart. I grew impatient at the Roadmaster's slow pace. I felt responsible for Beth's condition. Sins of omission, or commission, I wasn't sure which. Probably both.

Dr. Ramirez concentrated on his driving now and we didn't talk. Wind whipped against my face and tears burned in the corners of my eyes. Never did decide on an answer.

I sat on a flat rock under a gum tree that butted up against a dilapidated building which looked as though it had been a garage in a former life. It was late morning and the air had grown still. An old, yellow dog lay in the shade of a bungalow. He was as still as death, except that every now and then the tip of his tail twitched. In the wide blue bowl of a sky nothing moved, not even a cloud. Even the flies and bees were still.

I thought about Beth and Lexington and old Mr. Adams just east of Culpepper Street. One of his stories would have helped pass the time. One of his cold bottles of beer would have been better. Even though I knew I could never start drinking again, I wanted one more. That's the way it is when you're a drunk; you always want just one more.

Finally, an image of Preston crept out from whatever corner it had been hiding in and I shivered in spite of the heat. He had to be looking hard by now. A wild idea that he might recant and sic Lethridge on me bloomed. I studied it for a long time, but never figured out a way he could do it without exposing himself. My conclusion was not comforting. After some time, Lethridge began to appeal to me; at least with him I'd get a trial.

Finally the doctor came out. For a moment he stood with half his face shaded by a large gray-green shrub, while he held the flimsy screen door open as though uncertain whether to step outside or retreat into the house. Then he shook himself like a wet dog and let the screen door go bang behind him and walked slowly across the open ground to me.

I rose to greet him. Sweat dotted my palms and I wiped them on the outside of my trousers. Dr. Ramirez smiled up at me. One of his bicuspids was missing.

"How is she?"

He cleared his throat and pulled a pack of Camels out of his shirt pocket. When he had one lit, he took a puff and blew smoke out his nose and rubbed the toe of one of his scuffed wingtips through the soft soil.

"I know, I know. It is a filthy habit, especially problematic for a physician. After all, we are supposed to set the example of good health." He rolled his arms, turned his palms to the sun, and shrugged, "Still, we are only human, and all humans have vices. At least that is my theory and I am sticking to it." He cocked his head to one side and eyed me through the smoke. Sweat glistened on his forehead. "Do you have vices, señor?"

"Several,"

"Ah, you prove my point. As I think it says in the Bible, 'all have sinned and come short of the mark.'" The doctor shook himself again and pulled his body erect. The cigarette still dangled from the corner of his mouth and thin plumes of smoke drifted upward toward his squinting eyes. They were as impassive as dark stones. "I believe she has pneumonia. The strain that moves quickly inside the body."

"Dangerous?"

"Potentially. I have given her an injection, but," he shrugged, "who can say? In any case, she should be in a hospital. Do you have money?"

"Not much. A few pesos."

"Then it will have to be Sisters. Their equipment is dated and much used and there are no private rooms, but it is clean and I have a colleague who will help us. I will make arrangements for an ambulance. It should be here by three o'clock."

"Thank you."

"You are welcome. Also, you will get a bill from me and the ambulance service. Save your pesos for the hospital. They are enough to make a down payment. I have others to see and must go now. I will make the necessary telephone calls when I get back to my office."

He turned on his heel and started for the '58. Halfway there he stopped and turned around. Ramirez took the cigarette out of his mouth. "Tell me, señor, does your wife drink much?"

"Too much, every day."

The doctor dropped the cigarette and ground it out beneath his shoe. "That's what I thought, señor. Then I will wish you good luck. You will need it."

"Thanks, Doc."

I stood in the shade of the gum tree and watched until the '58 was out of sight and its dust trail had blended into the brown horizon. Then I crossed the courtyard and went over to the old dog. I bent down and rubbed the back of his neck and scratched him good behind the ears. He opened one baleful yellow eye. I gave him a final pat, stood up, and went inside to get Beth ready for the ambulance. Sunlight was very hot against my back and my throat was tight and dry.

The man who rode with us in the back of the ambulance was short and dark and spoke rapid-fire Spanish. Muscles stood out in his forearms as he maneuvered equipment and Beth.

In the back of the ambulance the air was cool. The drone of the air conditioning unit rose above the road noise, punctuated only by Beth's moans.

In spite of the injection, red splotches accented her cheekbones and her forehead was unnaturally warm against my lips. A few miles from the hospital her eyelids flickered, then came open. Her tongue slipped out and licked both lips. Cracks the thickness of a pencil mark ran through them. When she spoke her voice rattled in her throat like last year's cornhusks blowing in the wind.

"Where are we?"

"In an ambulance. Taking you to a hospital."

"I feel so awful, Frank. What's wrong with me?"

"The doctor says you have pneumonia."

"But my chest hurts so bad. Thought maybe it was a heart attack." Tears on her cheek matched the tears in her voice.

"That's the fluid buildup in your lungs. Doctor Ramirez thinks we need to get you to the hospital where they have equipment to drain that."

"Ramirez, he was the white-haired man who came to the house?"

"Yes."

"He looked at me so sadly. I'm going to die, aren't I, Frank?"

I looked over at the attendant. His eyes were on my face, but he said nothing. Then he averted his eyes. If he'd passed a message I missed it. His face was as smooth as polished walnut.

I turned back to Beth and ran the palm of my right hand across her cheek. My hand was so rough and callused that I was afraid it scratch her skin.

"Nonsense, you'll be fine. We just have to get you to the hospital, that's all."

Beth lifted the corners of her mouth. I figured it was the best she could do.

"You'll miss me when I am gone, won't you?" Her voice was so faint that it wasn't even a good whisper. I had to put my face very close to her mouth to hear.

Though the air conditioner still hummed, there was sweat on my upper lip and down the small of my back. I could hear Beth's faint gasps as she drew in air. Seemed to me as if she were trying to suck the last of the air out of the tiny cubicle.

"Baby, you'll outlive me," I said.

She closed her eyes, and, as if that simple act had generated energy, she upgraded her smile. "I love you, Frank Kohler. You should have been the best thing that ever happened to me. But you came too late. Too late, and as a lie. You and I both know that an alcoholic is always an alcoholic and that a liar is always a liar. So I know you're lying, Frank."

"Not this time. I love you, Beth. Truly."

"Enough to kill me, Frank?"

"That was a long time ago. In another life. I was another man."

"But you're still a liar. Yes, I know you say you love me, and that I believe. I love you, too. Love you the best I can. You should have known me in my prime."

"I did."

"No, you didn't." She spoke now in short bursts, punctuated by labored breathing. "You saw me. Seeing is not knowing. Awful truth of it is, Frank, that none of us really knows another person. Don't even really know ourselves." She paused and I watched her chest rise and fall. Pain dimmed her eyes, but she managed a fragile smile.

"Truth is just too awful to admit. So I'm a liar, too. But I do love you. Better than anything. Better than forever. And that's okay, because lies and loves go together. In fact, they are so intertwined that they can't exist without each other."

She placed a hand on her chest. Her skin was almost translucent. Bones and blue veins were running just below the skin. Pain crossed her face in a series of interconnected waves. Then she slitted her eyes open. "Now kiss me once, darling, before we get to the hospital. Just once, for all your love and all your lies."

Her eyelids fell shut and I bent and kissed her. Her lips were dry, yet yielding.

I kept the kiss short so she could breathe. Her gasps were plainly audible now above the drone of the air conditioner. I looked at the attendant. Our eyes met, but his told me nothing.

The ambulance made a long sweeping turn and he broke eye contact and glanced out the porthole. Then he got busy with the equipment. I shut my eyes, tightly, so that none of my tears would leak out. Most of them were for Beth, but a few were for me.

45

They came in the end. I knew they would.

Late in the afternoon of the second day my eyes picked Juan up as he rounded the corner, stepping out from the shadows of the feed store on the corner into the final light. He came with head down, neck bowed, placing his feet carefully. He moved like a tired, old man. Quite suddenly, I realized he was.

Darkness was already slipping into Beth's ground floor room. Juniper shadows were deep outside her window. Birds were calling to each other against the coming night. In her low-ceilinged room it was not quite dark. I sat silently on a plastic chair.

The old lady who had been in the other bed had died that morning. Her bed had been stripped and her clothes removed, but no one had taken her chart or given away her bed.

We were alone in the room. The only sound was the rhythmic shushing of the ventilator unit. Just enough light seeped into the room to allow me to see the rise and fall of Beth's chest. I sat and stared out the window at brick walls and Juan and the lengthening shadows. Juan disappeared into the deepening shadow and the birds fell silent.

He scratched at the door then pushed it open. As he pulled his wide-brimmed hat from his head his craggy face intruded into a light. It was coated with a thin layer of field dust. His eyes came to my face, then danced away.

"Amigo? Joe?"

"Sí."

"Is it all right to come in?"

"Sure, come on in. She's sleeping."

He walked across the clean, faded tile in dusty boots. For a moment I thought he might be going to shake hands, but instead he looked at his stained fists and thrust both into the pockets of his Levi's.

"How is she?" His voice was tired, but he held himself straight-backed with his chin up. In that moment I understood how he once went fifteen with Gomez in an outdoor arena in Tijuana in August."

"Holding her own. No more, no less."

Juan rubbed the back of one hand across his mouth. "What does the doctor say, amigo?"

"He says the medicine of man and Mexico have done what they can, and it is time for me to pray."

"Do you know the right prayers, hombre?"

"I have said all the prayers I know. We'll see if they're the right ones."

Juan moved from the side of the bed to the window. He stood perfectly still, staring into the blackness. Silence grew like a new planting between us. Finally, without looking at me, he said, "When my son died there were no right prayers."

"Perhaps there never are, amigo. In any case, the pneumonia will decide. Sorry to hear about your son. I did not know."

He nodded, somehow making the movement formal. "Pneumonia. My caballero, that can be very bad," he said.

"Very bad."

"Still, you have Doctor Ramirez. He is very good."

"He has been very kind. Tomorrow, or the day after, will tell us the rest. You look tired. Do you want to sit?"

Juan shook his head like a bull before the cape. "No, no. I can't stay. I must leave soon if I am to catch my ride."

"With who?"

"Tomas. He drives the bus to Tacopeka."

"Tall man with little hair?"

"Sí."

"Think I saw him at Fiesta. Someone told me he was a writer."

Juan snorted. "He is my wife's cousin who thinks he is a poet. He writes much, but little is published. He claims his lack of success is because his words are too full of meaning. I, myself, do not understand any of them."

Juan turned from the window and walked to the foot of Beth's bed. He looked at her face, and the mask over her mouth, and the plastic tubes running to and from her body. In the single shaft of light the workings of his face were plain. He turned toward me.

"This is a poor time to speak of such matters, but I have no other, *mi hermano*." He shaped the words until they were almost a question.

"I *comprende*. Go ahead."

"I hear things. I hear talk. People know that I have been places away from here and seen things which are not here. They know they can tell me things that they do not understand and that I may understand them."

"And?"

"They tell me that there are men, strangers, who ask after you and the lady." He nodded at Beth.

"How many men?"

"*Tres.*"

"What sort of men?"

"*Blanco.* From north of the border."

"How long have they been in town?"

Juan shrugged. "*Dos* days, maybe *tres.*"

"What do the people tell them?"

Juan fingered the brim of his hat. "I, myself, would tell them nothing. You understand that."

"*Sí.*"

"As for the others? Who can say?" he closed his eyes and fell silent. After a minute, he opened them, blinking a little. "You are not surprised?"

"No. I knew they would come. In the end they had to come. You see, they had no choice. Only questions were where and when."

"Then I understand. I must go now or I will miss my ride. It is a long walk home for an old man."

"Not too long for a tough old man who once went the distance with Gomez."

"That was many years ago," Juan said.

"Your heart is still full of courage," I said.

"Perhaps, but my legs are gone."

"So are mine, amigo. Guess I'll just have to stand and fight."

With a sudden movement Juan came around the bed and stood before me, revealing a vision of the quickness that had been his calling card. He hesitated a second, then put out his hand. I shook it. It was full of calluses and bones. Muscles in his forearm ran long and hard all the way to his elbow.

"May fortune be with you, hombre." He put his hat back on his head.

"*Gracias.* Juan?"

He turned. The shaft of light that slid in from the hall highlighted his face. "*Sí?*"

"Thanks. For everything."

"*De nada.*"

I sat alone in the room with Beth and listened to the ventilator and watched her chest rise and fall and the liquid flow back and forth in the tubes. I thought back to that night of the liquor store fiasco. I thought real hard. No matter how you rearranged the pieces they always added up the same. Witnesses said I was there; I knew I couldn't have been. I didn't even own a gun. My lousy past was catching up with me. I'd heard the rumor that it did that. Confirming it brought zero satisfaction.

Until the shifts changed, I ruminated about the trio of strangers and what they might have planned and what my options were. The new nurse was plump and dark and pretty. She smiled at me when she came into the room. While she checked the gently throbbing machines, I got up and went down the hall to the small cantina next to the newsstand.

The cantina was nearly full of people who wore long faces and talked in low tones. The newsstand was closed for the night. I bought a ham sandwich and a cup of coffee. The bread was dry. The coffee black and bitter as a broken promise.

Disembodied voices drifted in from the hallway, I caught irregular patches of provincial dialects. Rhythms of words rose and fell, tinged with a baroque beauty.

By midnight my head was pounding in syncopation to the heartbeats of the ventilation machine. I tried to wash my headache away with lukewarm coffee and conversation with the son of the old man in room 37.

The man had been diagnosed with pancreatic cancer, and he and his son passed the nights sipping on whiskey. They spoke in bursts that came and went like spastic flashes of heat lightning. Most of each night they stared silently at each other, smiling faintly between sips of raw whiskey.

About a quarter after twelve, the son, who looked about forty, came out in the hall and told me his father was dying. He stood with his back against the lime green plaster walls and sipped from his Dixie cup and let twin trails of tears travel down the grooves of his cheeks. I told him I was sorry. He smiled and nodded his big knobby head. Kind words are the cheap currency of dark, hospital nights.

Beth's regular nurse came at one and three. The head nurse came at five. Both wore starched expressions and neither would look me in the eye. I couldn't ask them the question I didn't really need answered. So I sat without speaking in the half-light and sipped half-cold coffee and watched dying dreams slow dance inside my brain. Sometime after five I slept.

I awoke with morning sun in my face and a bitter aftertaste in my mouth. Dr. Ramirez, a younger colleague, and the head nurse were in the room. The two physicians studied Beth's chart. The nurse studied the tops of her white shoes.

I sat up, sloshing the contents of my Styrofoam cup across the faded fabric of my jeans. The coffee had gone cold and I was instantly aware of my unshaven face and unwashed body. My breath was foul in my mouth and my voice rasped in my throat.

"How is she?"

Dr. Ramirez turned his large head and looked down on me. His eyes were sunk deep in his head. He did not recognize me. Then, remembrance dawned. The doctor spread his arms at his sides, palms turned up. "Ah, so sorry, señor. Please forgive me. Such a night it has been." Ramirez inclined his head toward the bed. "Your lady, she did not lose any ground during the night."

I tried to read his eyes, but they gave nothing away. "Did she gain any?" I finally asked.

He shook his massive skull. Veins pulsed just beneath skin stretched drumhead taut across his temples. "No, neither did she gain any ground."

The younger man edged closer to Dr. Ramirez and murmured words I couldn't quite catch. The older man listened with eyes half-closed. His hands were busy in a pocket of his smock. Sweat stained the valleys of his arms and drops of dried blood clotted the once white smock. The hair on his arms was short black curling wires.

"My colleague, Dr. Fuentes, reminds me that we will try a new antibiotic this morning, *una inyeccion*. He tells me they had some success with it in similar cases in Mexico City."

My throat suddenly seemed very dry. "Much success?" I asked.

The two physicians exchanged glances. The younger doctor shrugged his shoulders in a self-deprecating way.

"*Un poco*, a little success," Dr. Ramirez said.

"Thank you," I said. Then I turned and looked across Beth and out the window. Sunlight fell against white walls of buildings across the street. The buildings stood quite close together as though they had been built more with defense in mind than functionality. The sky was high and flat and cobalt blue. A single jet stream wormed its white way north. Shadows beneath the junipers were long and thin, and stretched until they broke against the cracked black asphalt of the road that bisected the town square.

Dr. Ramirez dropped a hand on my shoulder and gently rubbed it back and forth. "We are trying, my amigo. We have yet to accomplish much, but we are trying very hard. Modern medicine may be marvelous, but it is not so marvelous as God above. There are times when He allows us to assist. Other times He makes the final diagnosis. And who among us can say how it will then go?"

His words were so many drops of rain. I sat very still and watched juniper shadows thicken and lengthen. In a little while the doctors and the nurse went away and I could again hear the hushed sucking hiss of the ventilator. All morning the nurses came and went and the shadows grew until they covered the street and impaled themselves on the white walls of the buildings that lined the road.

46

Around noon Beth's eyes flickered. The movement wrenched me out of my chair. By the time I'd crossed over to her bed both eyes were open. They were grandmother eyes now, faded, washed-out. She blinked, trying to bring them into focus. I think she recognized me and tried to speak. Inarticulate sounds maneuvered around the ventilation unit. Her fingers were wounded butterflies fluttering against the white sheets. I squeezed both her hands between mine. Then I ran for the nurse.

I found her, finally, giving a fattish young man a sponge bath. By the time I made her understand the significance of the events in Room 34 and convinced her to follow me several precious moments were forever lost.

The moment we entered the room I knew Beth had drifted back into unconsciousness. I knew from the way she lay like a rag doll with the insides all sucked out. The nurse checked her pulse, lifted an eyelid, adjusted the ventilation machine, then turned to me.

"Señor, she is unconscious. Are you sure you saw her eyes open?" She glanced at the chair I'd been sitting in. A pillow was propped against the back and a worn, green blanket was draped across an arm. "There are times when dreams seem as real as life."

"Yes, I know, but her eyes were open. I was not sleeping. I was standing as close to her as you are. I saw her eyes open and her fingers move. She recognized me. Sorry to have troubled you. I just thought it was a good sign."

"It may have been," the nurse said.

"What do you mean, it may have been? Why wouldn't it have been a good sign?"

She shrugged and did bird wings with her hands. "Sometimes that is the way they announce they are through the crisis. Then, soon, they are on the road to recovery."

I stepped across the floor until I could count the pores of her face. Her eyes were only mirrors. "You said sometimes," I said. "What about the other times? What does it mean then?"

She was silent for so long that the quiet in the room grew painful. We were so close I could hear her breathe. She put her right hand on my left shoulder. It was a small hand, ringless, with manicured nails. For such a small hand it was very heavy.

"There are times, señor, when they seem to rally. Only it is a false rally, a final glimmer of life before the end."

"Death?"

"Si. It is as if God grants them a final moment. I have seen it many times. Always the patient is lucid, in full possession of themselves, and free of pain. Such moments are brief. Many last only a few seconds. They are beautiful to behold. A memory to treasure forever."

I didn't want to hear any more about memories to treasure. My mind was already full of memories I wanted to expunge. Memories can be bastards.

I turned and walked until I stood in front of the window. I put my face in my hands. "Go now," I said. "Please. Please go away."

In a few seconds I heard the door close. I stood in front of the window, seeing nothing, until the attendant came to clean the room at one o'clock.

47

Coffee was going cold in my cup and the afternoon was rapidly fading. Beth lay silently, curled up small. I pushed up from my chair and went back to my post at the window.

By now the sun was low against the western horizon. The heat of the day had passed and people had begun to venture out. The advance guard of the evening promenade had begun to form in the triplicate shadows of the town's only multi-story buildings: the bank, a branch of the biggest chain department store in Mexico, and an office building for a firm that specialized in petro-chemicals and cotton.

One man walked against the human tide. He moved with a deliberate stride that looked familiar. His down-turned face was wreathed in shadows cast by his sombrero. Despite the shadows, I knew him. Juan broke from the crowd and angled across the street toward the hospital.

His clothes were dusty and his machete hung in a scabbard from his waist. His dark face glistened with sweat. He came on steadily, then stopped in the shade of the largest juniper. After glancing left, then right, he turned his face up to me. His eyes found mine and he made a quick, almost imperceptible jerk of his head. I caught the message in the movement and turned from the window.

After the air conditioning of the hospital the late afternoon was like the afterblast of a furnace. Before I could go down the three concrete steps and cross the twenty yards of open ground my shirt was plastered to my back.

"You came directly from the fields, amigo," I said.

"There was no time to change."

"What's the matter?"

Juan wiped the sweat from his forehead. His fingers left damp tracks. "The men who are looking for you were at the ranch today.

They asked many questions of many people. They also talked among themselves. They assumed we were all ignorant but my English was far superior to their Spanish. Their words were not kind."

Juan put a hand on my shoulder. I could smell onions on his breath and see the network of scars at the corners of his eyes. "Amigo, they mean great harm to you and your lady, and there are those who would help them. Not for lack of love for you, you understand. But because they love pesos more. The norteamericanos who are looking for you have many pesos."

My head was starting to ache. "Do you know where they are?"

"Sí. Even now, they sit at the cantina *Santa Anna* talking with Rueben. A couple of drinks and a handful of pesos and he will tell them all he knows, and more."

Thought patterns formed, mutated in geometric progression, then exploded. My knees seemed strangely weak and I felt faint. I shook my body like an old dog, reminding myself of Dr. Ramirez. The doctor was a good man and had done all he could. However, he couldn't save Beth and he couldn't save me. I couldn't even save myself.

"Will you help me?" I asked.

"Sí. Those men are arrogant and ignorant. That is not a good combination. Besides, you are my amigo. We have worked together, side by side, in the fields. You have treated me as a *caballero*, one just like yourself."

"*Gracias*. We must move quickly," I said. "They will find me soon, anyway. This town is too small to hide in. Besides," I nodded at the building where a small body lay in a large bed, "I cannot run. Therefore, I must meet them on my ground, at my time.

I will be at the Rock of the Angels at five o'clock tomorrow afternoon. Tell them to come on the Juarez Road. They can see the rock for miles, but they will have to walk the last five hundred yards. They will have to come up the hill to me."

"What will you do when they come?"

I shrugged the Latin shrug I'd learned in Mexico. "We will talk. If reason does not prevail then it is as good a place as any to make a stand. If I remember correctly, there are many paths and many large rocks."

"Sí, that is correct. How do you know the terrain so intimately?"

"My Sundays have been my own and your country is very beautiful. Rugged, but gorgeous."

"Like our women?"

I laughed in spite of myself. "Your wits are still about you, Juan, even in the midst of a crisis."

"You forget, amigo. I had to enter the ring with Gomez in front of thousands with only boxing gloves. Gomez was one tough hombre. His head and hands were both made of stone."

"You said was, Juan. What happened to Gomez?"

"He was very tough, señor, but not so tough as a bullet. A young boy shot him in Guadalajara. Gomez was hurting the boy's little sister."

I nodded. "Go now while there is still time."

"Sí. I will go. Do you want me with you tomorrow?"

"I could not ask it."

Juan nodded his scarred head. "You have chosen well, hombre. The sun will be in their eyes."

"I hope it puts fear in their hearts. If the day goes badly, will you do what you can for my lady?"

"Gladly."

"Go now."

Juan reached inside his loose shirt and pulled out a roll of blue cloth. He unrolled it and offered it to me. A bolo knife gleamed from the inner folds of the fabric. Final rays of the dying sun glittered on the blade. I took the knife and ran a finger along the edge. It was very sharp. A drop of my blood stained the metal. Carefully I licked at the crimson. It was a perverted communion.

"*Gracias*, amigo."

"*De nada*." Juan turned and walked away from the deep shade of the junipers. At the edge of the road he turned and raised a hand. Then he jogged across the road and was swallowed up by the crowd. For a few seconds I could still see his sombrero bobbing through the moving sea. When I could no longer mark his progress, I wrapped the cloth around the knife and began walking toward the *Cantina Santa Anna*. I walked slowly, mingling with the crowd. I chose the long way around.

Aromas of cooking onions and beans and rice settled over the street like a low-hanging fog. My mouth watered. I realized I hadn't eaten all day.

On a darkened balcony above someone strummed a guitar. Plants and small shrubs lined the balcony so thickly that it was impossible to tell where one began or another ended. The guitar player was no more than just another shadowy blur against the night sky.

A couple of blocks over a mariachi band tuned up. A scraggly looking cat crossed the street before me, carrying his tattered tail high. The arch in his back was regal. A dog growled low in his throat from beyond a sagging wrought iron fence.

I crossed at the corner of Valdez and Ensenada. Now there was one streetlight per block and it was easy to stay in the shadows. I stepped on a piece of rotting fruit. At the end of the block, where the shadows were deepest, I stumbled over a body. I caught myself against the corner of a fruit bin and whispered, "Pardon, *por favor*." A man grunted drunkenly and rolled over.

I came up on the backside of the *Santa Anna* with the night breeze in my face, creeping among the tombstones of the churchyard that lay on the far side of a narrow alley. Massive adobe church walls threw shadows as dark and deep as canyons. I kept flicking my eyes to the lights of the cantina ahead. Tombstone marble was smooth and cool beneath my fingers.

The alley that ran behind the *Santa Anna* was no more than ten yards wide. I duck-walked across it and put my face against the rough wall that enclosed the cantina. I counted to sixty, then raised my head.

Ten yards from me four men talked in hushed tones. A half dozen bottles sat on the table before them. Even though I'd known he would be there, it was a shock to see Preston's polished, tanned face. There was more silver at his temples than I remembered. Les was on his left and my old buddy Joe from the car ride to Juarez sat on his right with a bottle in his hand. That trip seemed to have happened so long ago that another man might well have made it.

Rueben had his back to me and he was talking, very rapidly, throwing in hand gestures for free. He spoke just too low for me to understand his words.

I leaned against the wall, risking a look now and then. The breeze blew cool across the damp hairs at the base of my neck. I was almost beyond hungry, but the smell of the beer was exquisite torture. Certain desires never die. Right now I wanted a drink and to go on living.

After one more round, Juan emerged from the kitchen door. I watched him make eye contact with Rueben. I didn't catch the sign, but Rueben pushed away from the table. I hoped Juan had gotten the story straight. I gave him ten minutes and recrossed the alley. Tombstones rose from the dusty earth like stone men. Lighted cantina lanterns swung in the evening breeze.

48

Old 65 rumbled into town just before five o'clock and woke me from a fitful sleep full of disjointed dreams. It was a local, making a stop at every hamlet between the Rio Verde and the coast. Clanging and banging punctured the silence as workers loaded fruits and vegetables and bleating goats and clay pots as big as a man's torso. Passengers murmured as they boarded and engines hissed.

I stood up, stretched, and walked to the window. Outside, darkness still held, but I could sense the pre-dawn promise of another sunrise. Life was suddenly a profoundly sweet taste on my tongue and I realized with a jolt that I wasn't ready to let go.

Beth looked incredibly pale and weak lying on her narrow hospital bed. Her chest rose and fell with the rhythm of the machine. All life seemed to have drained from her body so that it was only by the pulsing fluids in the tubes that ran from IV units into her arms that she was sustained. Her hands were cold to the touch and her face void of expression. Gazing at her, I thought about what I had and what I had lost and what I still had to lose. Then I said the best prayer I knew, fearing it wasn't going to be enough.

I kissed her cheeks and lips.

Her eyelids flickered, but maybe that was my imagination.

When they did I whispered her name, and told her that I loved her. Heading for the door I wondered if I would see her alive again. Like Frost had written, I had miles to go and promises to keep, and I needed the sun in their eyes, not mine.

Gold rimmed the eastern horizon when I reached the broken boulders and scrub pines that lined the narrow path at the base of the mountain. As far as I could see the trail wound steeply among ever larger rocks and increasingly smaller trees. I could not see the end of the trail.

I ate half of one of the two Hershey bars I'd liberated from the nurse's station and took a swallow from a plastic bottle of filtered water fresh from Guadalajara, by way of the hospital refrigerator. I had one in reserve. Already the water was warm. Behind me, shrouded in mist, the town lay sleeping. I capped the bottle, stuck the rest of the candy bar in my shirt pocket, and started up the path. A long walk loomed before me, and perhaps death was waiting at the end. But none of that mattered; it was a walk I had to make if I wanted to be able to live with myself.

By mid-morning I'd reached the upper edge of the tree line. Wind was cool on my face. I ate the second half of the first candy bar and drank more water. At noon it was bare rocks, warm water, and half-melted chocolate, with the town splayed out before me in the valley below like far-flung toys of an angry child. By mid-afternoon I was where I wanted to be. They would come up the other way, where the road was passable for better than half the trip, but I had secured the high ground. The natives called it the Rock of the Angels. And there was beauty here, of a very rugged sort.

Half an hour of searching turned up three acceptable alternatives. I chose a jagged seam in a boulder the size of a small house. Sliding down into the dark wedge and putting my back against the smooth stone, I wondered at the force that had created a cleft in such a mammoth slab. Then I said another prayer. I said it for Beth and Juan and Reuben and Mike at the Final Furlong and Mrs. Hopkins and Ralph Adams and for my neighbor Jerry, and even for Juanita the whore of Juarez who had given me her body when that was all she had to give, and, finally, for myself. I hadn't often been a good man and it had been a damn long time since I'd darkened a church door, but maybe God would still show a poor sinner a little mercy. I figured to need all the help I could get.

Surrounded on three sides by rock, I had a narrow view of the steep trail just as it crested and flattened out. Only directly from the front could anyone see me, and even then I would be distorted by shadows and reflected light. At the appointed time I'd be in deep shadow and they would be staring directly into the setting sun. I drank all but a final swallow of my water and laid the bolo knife on the stone before me. Its blade gleamed.

The afternoon grew up and moved behind me. Sunlight burned the back of my neck. I ate the last square of candy and licked the paper clean. Then I swallowed the last of the water. I wished I had brought more of both. I also had plenty of time to wish I'd lived my life differently. Guess I'd finally changed, and maybe for the better, but I'd left it powerfully late in the game. Comeback kids don't always win.

Hazy recollections of an old philosophy course drifted to me on the thin air. One philosophy, I couldn't recall the name, espoused the theory that everything that occurred in your life happened for a reason, because it was supposed to, because it was what you really wanted down deep. In college I hadn't bought that. Facing death alone on a mountain in Mexico I still didn't buy it.

About four o'clock the wind abruptly died off. The mountains grew conspicuously still and hot. In twenty minutes I was damp inside my shirt. More than ever I wanted water.

With the abatement of the wind, I could hear furtive scurrying among the rocks. Lizards thrived in this country and there figured to be snakes. The sounds were small and non-threatening, in a way oddly comforting.

Once I heard the high shrill cry of a hawk. I searched the unending curved blue sky until I found him. Almost directly above me, he was soaring on the thermals in ever-widening circles. Remembering other dark birds, I watched him until he was only a black speck drifting hundreds of feet above the valley floor.

Gradually the afternoon became soft and warm and gentle as an old shawl on my shoulder. As hospital nights caught up with me my eyelids became incessantly heavy. Closing my eyes, I thought about

Beth. Then she drifted away and half-asleep, I floated into a twilight zone of the amazing mind.

Voices in the rocks pulled me back into Mexico. I blinked my eyes open and reached for the bolo knife. It seemed strangely heavy. Tremblings ran through my arm like chilled electricity.

The voices were closer now, swirling and tumbling over each other, and I could pick up snatches of conversation. "Damn, I'm tired" and "How much farther?" and "That bastard, Kohler" rose more clearly than the rest through the pellucid air.

Pushing my back off the rock wall, I crawled to the front of the shadows. Keeping my face well within their darkness I peered down the trail. For perhaps fifteen yards I could see clearly before the trail broke sharply to the left and bent downhill. Rocks seemed alive with sounds of men climbing and echoes of their conversations. Muscles knotted with tension. Shivers ran up and down my spine like alternating current. My left leg quivered uncontrollably.

Without warning, shadows of men danced before me on the rock walls. I could see three, one separated by a couple of yards from the other two, who wavered so closely together that they were almost one. Shadows rose and fell as the men climbed upward.

"Frank, hey Frank! You up here? You'd better be up here after all this climbing." I recognized the voice. For four years I'd heard it virtually every day. My old Kentucky teammate. Now, just like me, another fool one hell of a long way from gridiron glory. Press stepped into the sunlight.

"That's far enough, Press. I can see you fine. Now tell me what you want."

He shaded his eyes with his hands and squinted against the sun. His blue and red flannel shirt was unbuttoned and swung loosely with his movements. The wind had sprung back to life in the past few minutes and it fluttered at his hair. "Come on out, Frank. Let's talk out in the open."

"I like it the way it is," I said.

"Come on, now. Old friends should speak face to face."

"You've come a long way, Press. You didn't come that far just to chat."

He was listening very intently, trying to locate me. I glanced at the other two men, Les Johnson, looming huge as a thunderstorm, and my old buddy, Juarez Joe. Sweat glistened on their faces and metal glittered in their hands. I shivered like a scared dog.

Press took a step forward, moving in my direction. Now he was ten yards away. "We need to talk, Frank. Talk about business. Unfinished business."

"Tell your friends to go back down the hill."

He nodded and waved at the two men who stood in the curve of the trail. They took a couple of steps back, but Preston came a step closer. Sunlight was still in his eyes, soon it would drop below the pyramid of rocks that rose like a stone cathedral behind me.

"No need to come any closer, Press," I said. "Say what you've got to say."

He took another step. I gripped the knife handle so tightly my hand hurt.

"All right," he said, "you were supposed to do a job for me, Frank. One for your old teammate. Word is it didn't get done. Can't tell you how disappointed I am in you, Frank."

"Then why bother? Turn around and go back to Kentucky. We'll stay down here in Mexico and everybody can live happily ever after."

"You're too damn old to believe in fairy tales, Frank. Life doesn't work that way. I can't just let this ride."

"Why not?" Shadows were beginning to shift on me and I inched to my right.

Press shook his handsome head. In that moment he looked like a frustrated old psychology professor I'd had at UK by the name of Carner. He'd been from Mississippi and was inordinately fond of quoting Faulkner. Funny what insignificant thoughts cross a man's mind when he thinks he might die.

"I've got a life in Kentucky, Frank. I have important friends, and I'm running for senator. America needs me. My ideas can make a difference. But I can't make senator with a missing wife who just wandered into the land of the Aztecs with an old football buddy turned boozehound. My important friends don't like a missing alcoholic bimbette. A tragic, too-early death they can understand. Even wins me the sympathy vote. I need my friends, Frank."

"You mean you need their money, Press. Do all your friends have to have money?"

"No, but it helps. Now come on out, Frank. We need to talk about Beth. You need to tell me where she is. Unpleasant action is sometimes necessary. Let's make it as easy on ourselves as possible." His voice was smooth. It turned my stomach.

I could no longer see Les or Joe. The sunlight had fallen below Preston's eyes. There were sounds in the rocks that rose to my right and I could see flickers of movement below, off to my left. I felt a sudden empathy for General George Armstrong Custer.

"What kind of unpleasant action, Press? Quit moving, you're close enough."

"I need to finalize the plans we made. My career depends on it, the rest of my life. Perhaps our country's future. Surely you understand that. Now, tell me where Beth is."

"Beth is very sick, Press. She's dying."

"Bullshit. Surely you don't expect me to believe that crap?"

I hadn't; some people live lies so deeply they never quite recognize the truth.

I kept watching Press, focusing on his eyes and his hands. On both sides noises were louder now. I risked a quick glance up to my right. When I looked back the automatic was in Press's right hand. The black hole of the barrel looked as wide and deep as eternity. There was something I had to know before it was too late.

"One thing, Press?"

"Yeah, what's that?"

"How did you do it? How'd you set me up."

He laughed. In the thin air the laughter had a hollow ring. "I wondered if you would ever figure it out, you dumb fuck."

Press shook his head. In the failing light he was quite handsome. Handsome in a tragic way, Press made me think of a certain Roman emperor.

"Nothing went quite right that night. I needed to get something to hold over you and a rather disreputable character I know owed me major cash. He couldn't pay, but was willing to perform a favor to get back to even. We were going to get you wasted, then borrow the taxi and do the holdup. He had experience along that line and it was all planned out to the minute.

You screwed things up, Frank, you know that?" The knockout pill was in that last whiskey, but you never got around to drinking it. In fact, you gave me the slip for a while. Pissed me off, not to mention scaring the crap out of me. Had to scramble like hell and take way more chances than I liked. Borrowing the taxi after you'd made it home was a risk, but I had to take it."

His mouth rearranged itself into a crooked grin. "Still it would have been alright, except for the shooting. Want you to know, Frank, that wasn't part of the plan. Guess numbnuts just panicked. He was supposed to grab a few bucks and run, then make sure his license plates were visible. That was all. I don't like to kill, you know."

He quit talking then. Silence encased the top of the mountain. I spoke against that silence. "Unless you have to, right? Like with Beth. Isn't that right, you son-of-a-bitch?"

Wind whined among the boulders.

"But why, Press? Why all this? Why not just a divorce?"

"Divorces cost votes. For a relic, the old senator is one tough man to beat. Just ask the three that tried."

"Okay, but surely being U.S. Senator isn't worth Beth's life."

"Beth is a burden, a fat, drunk, over-sexed burden. And I have debts to pay. Big debts to powerful people. This was my big chance to repay those debts and give myself a real future. Life had gotten boring, real boring." His eyes roomed the rocks. "Guess, to tell the truth, I missed the limelight a little."

He smiled as though something funny had occurred to him. "Never mind, Frank, you always were number two. You'd never understand."

I stared at Press, and beyond, into the overarching blue nothingness. "No, I wouldn't," I said. The air around me seemed extraordinarily clear, so clear that it made my head hurt.

Press was still smiling. At least his lips were parted and his teeth were white in the dying rays of the sun. The knife felt small and inadequate. Just like college, I was running second string. I wished I had a gun. All my life I'd been wishing for things. Wishing was for fools. That much I'd learned. Only it looked like I'd learned it too late.

"Might as well come out, Frank. I know where you are. Maybe I can't see you right now, but I can guess real close. In five minutes I'll see your shadow. You can't go anywhere, you big dumb fullback. You've got yourself trapped with no way out. So tell me where Beth is and I'll have the rest taken care of. Then you can drink yourself to death."

"Go to hell."

Preston fired at the sound of my voice. The bullet chipped at the stone wall two feet away from my head. My body trembled. It felt far away, disconnected, as though it belonged to another man.

"It's just a matter of time, Frank. You might as well talk." He took a quick step toward me and fired again. The bullet burned a shallow path along the outside of my left arm and I grunted through gritted teeth. I crouched lower and turned the knife so the blade would come up from below. Aim for his gut, just like in the movies. Problem was I was no celluloid hero.

Another step. He was so close I could see his fingers on the trigger and sweat beads that dotted his upper lip. I wondered if he could smell my fear, or my dripping blood. I watched the lights in his eyes. When they started to dim I would go with the knife.

"That is far enough, señor," said a new voice. It was an old voice, a familiar voice, floating from higher up and to my right. "Do not take another step. I have you covered. Back up and tell your friends to go back down the hill. This is not a good place to die."

"Who the hell are you?" Preston asked. If there was an element of fear in his voice I couldn't detect it. In his own way he'd always been a hard man. I hadn't realized how hard. In the end I'd underestimated him.

"A friend of your enemy," said the voice from the rocks. "Do not worry about me. Worry about yourself. That is enough. Now back up."

"Show yourself."

"Sorry, señor. I do not think so."

"Then your friend will have to die." Preston turned and fired. The bullet buzzed so closely by my head that I felt displaced air wash across my temple. Something large and dark and round flew from the rocks above. There was a thud and Preston roared in pain. I jumped from the shadows and flung myself at the gun in his hand.

He was as strong as I remembered. I got one hand on his forearm, but he got his free hand on my wrist above the knife. We danced a macabre pirouette across the narrow trail and onto an outcropping of rock. Loose stones shifted beneath my feet.

I twisted his wrist, and he bull-rushed me into a solid wall of stone. The knife flew from my hand and we staggered apart. I could hear the gun clatter down the rocky slope.

"No way, you bastard," he panted. In the aftermath of his words our breathing was audible. We were panting like a pair of rogue rhinos. I sucked in a lungful of air.

"Tell me where Beth is."

"No."

"Tell me!"

"Give it up, Press."

"I came to kill you and I will." His mouth was open and blood smeared his lower lip. His fine features were twisted. Sweat dripped off his face and onto mine.

I circled slowly to my left, trying to work my way over to the knife. All I could see was Press and sky and I was suddenly conscious of the end of the rocky outcropping behind me. Beyond was only the sheer drop of hundreds of feet to the rocks below. Sweat slickened my palms.

"It doesn't have to be, Press," I grunted. "Go on back home. Forget about us. Beth and I are just two poor rats trapped forever in Mexico."

He spoke through gritted teeth. "You're right about being in Mexico forever. Only you're going to be dead. I've got too much to lose to let either of you live. I hate it, old buddy, but it's simply a fact. The election depends on your death, and so does my future."

He gave me a sudden smile, and it was halftime of the Mississippi State game all over. Then he charged at me, roaring like some wild animal.

Instinctively, I took a step back in response and felt my footing go. I was falling through space. Everything seemed to move in slow motion. His voice was loud in my ear. I got one hand on his shirt as I smacked onto rocks. He seemed to float above me. For a second the flannel held, then it ripped off in a jagged patch.

His screams lingered in the thin air long after the body had disappeared.

Blood flowed down my face. I wiped it out of my eyes as I struggled to my feet. Ten feet away, Les and Joe stood before me. Each had a gun in one hand. The guns were big and black. I was too tired to do more than stare at them. I felt like a cornered coyote.

I tried to read their faces, but they were as expressionless as the wall of white stone towering above us. The air was as quiet as clouds. I could hear myself breathing, wondering with each breath if it would be my last. Suddenly I wondered what sort of man I might have been. Then I thought of Beth. I wanted to cry, but there was no future in tears, no honor. Honor was about all I had left.

Les cleared his throat.

"It was Press's play all the way, man. We've got no bone to pick with you. Joe and I are out of Mexico by tomorrow night. Way I'll tell the media, we saw nothing, heard nothing, know nothing. Press went off on a personal hiking trip. Wanted to get away from the campaign pressure for a couple of days. Planned to fly back later. You cool with that?"

My throat was painfully dry. I didn't trust my voice. My heart was still pounding wildly in my heaving chest. I nodded. For a moment we just stared at each other. I wondered what they were thinking. I was too scared to think. Then they lowered their guns and turned.

With the wind against my face, I watched them go down the hill, growing smaller and smaller, until they were only stick men. I did not look away until they were out of sight.

There was a noise behind me and I turned to meet it. Juan's lined face was broken into the most beautiful, horrible, gap-toothed grin I'd ever seen. I gave him my hand. It was only trembling a little, and I was proud of that.

"Thank you, amigo. You saved my life."

"It was nothing."

"Nothing, hell! I'd be dead if it weren't for you. I can never thank you enough."

"I knew you were outnumbered, and they let me see their guns at the cantina. Your bolo knife wasn't enough."

"How in hell did you get up here? I never heard you come. That was a hell of a walk for an old man."

Juan grinned even wider. "That was nothing. You forget I went fifteen with Gomez in Tijuana in August. Now that was something."

I laughed at him, and at the mountains, and at death on the valley floor below. Then I wiped a drying ribbon of blood off my face and put one arm around his shoulders and we started down the trail together in the gathering darkness.

I felt like I had just gone fifteen rounds with Gomez myself. Only now I going someplace I wished I didn't have to go. I was happy to be alive, yet knowing what awaited in the town far below, sad too. The sad you get when you hate what lies before you, but you can't do a damn thing about it. Sadness beyond grief.

My legs were weak and I stumbled now and then, catching myself on stones as old as the earth itself, leaning a little on Juan in the flat places, and trying not to cry. I felt like an old man, a poor old pitiful used-up relic of a man.

Still, I was glad to be alive. I was glad I was sober. I was glad Juan was with me. I was glad for the purple haze and the call of an unseen bird of the evening. I was glad I was tired. It meant I was alive. We slogged on through the gathering dark, tired fighters who still had one more round to go.

49

A man sat on the hospital steps, his left hand encased in a clean white bandage. His face was pointed straight ahead, eyes staring at everyone and everything that passed, seeing nothing. I climbed past him and went up the stairs and into the hospital.

The walls were still bilious green plaster. A chunk had peeled away above the admittance window. The waiting benches were lined with poor, sick people. One woman wore no shoes. Another nursed a baby at her brown breast. A little dark-eyed girl sat on the floor licking at a sucker. As I walked by she grinned at me. I couldn't see a tooth in her head.

The head nurse was coming out of room 34. She looked tired. When she noticed me she stopped and closed her face until it was a fist with hard black eyes.

"*Buenos dias,*" she said.

"*Buenos dias,*" I replied.

"We have missed you, señor." Her eyes changed as they noted the dirt on my hands and line of dried blood on my face.

"I had business. How is she?"

The nurse closed her eyes for a moment. When she opened them she said, "The doctor, he is discouraged."

"Is there hope?"

She shrugged. "Who can say?"

I could see it was the best the woman could say. "Is she suffering?"

Her eyes found mine. For several seconds we stared at each other. Then she looked away and said, "When the señora is conscious, there is pain."

"I see," I said. "Thank you."

"You are welcome." She turned and started walking. Five yards down the hall she stopped and turned back. "Señor?"

196

"Yes."

"Sometimes." She searched for the right words.

"Yes."

"There are times when the doctor can only do so much with medicine. You understand?"

I nodded, opened the door and stepped into Beth's room. I closed the door behind me. The click of the lock was sharp and loud.

Feeling like a vagrant ghost, I crossed the room and stood in the diffused sunlight that haloed the bed. Beth's eyes were closed, but her head was turned toward me as though she had been waiting for my return. She looked smaller than I remembered and her bones appeared more prominent.

Shifting the tubes, I crawled into the bed with her. I whispered her name and told her I loved her. I kissed her forehead, and eyes, and lips.

Her eyelids fluttered and then she was there in the room with me. She tried to find a smile and her lips moved, allowing whispers to escape. Perhaps it was only my imagination, but I thought she said, "I love you, Frank."

I held her soft body and stared into her eyes.

Time had no meaning. It felt as if that dimension had ceased to exist.

Somewhere in the quiet of late afternoon I felt her shudder, once, twice.

When the last of the light faded from her eyes, I kissed them shut.

Only then did I let the tears fall.

When darkness in the room was thick, I laid her head on the pillow and went to find the nurse. I could not make myself say goodbye. As I neared the nurse's station I saw Juan sitting on a wooden bench in the waiting room. I raised my hand and he gave me a sloppy salute. He tried to smile, but he simply looked tired.

I spoke in hushed tones to the nurse on duty. She was young and pretty and tears formed quickly in her dark brown eyes.

"I'm sorry, señor. Are you sure?"

"Yes."

She nodded. "We will take care of the rest."

"Thank you. I'll be back tomorrow," I said. Then I walked down the hall with the peeling bilious green plaster and out the front door into a soft, sweet, velvet blackness.

Moonlight lay silver on the junipers and the sweet scent of jasmine christened the air. For some time I stood on the steps and stared at the yellow street lamps, breathing deeply, trying to remember and forget all at the same time.

By the time I'd drifted back Juan had joined me. He looked at me and I shook my head. He bowed his for a moment and then we stepped together down the black ribbon of asphalt toward the village, an adobe bungalow full of memories, and Beth's meager possessions.

Crossing the hospital grounds I was struck with the sense that something inside me had died and now something new was being born to fill the void. I was tempted to stop and figure out the essence of the new elements, but my mind was too full of blood and death and grief to function. In the morning I would think on such things. To some degree, I would be a different man then, perhaps even a better one. Certainly, I had changed. I was no longer the man who spent hot August watching my life slip away at a crummy bar in Kentucky. Time and willpower would reveal the man I would become.

But not tonight. Today was still too much with me and my mind felt like a glass bowl that had been smashed against a wall of stone. It would take time to put all the fragments together. We crossed the street and turned into the night wind.

It promised to be a long walk to an empty shack and I wasn't sure I wanted to make the journey. Part of me wanted to start running, and keep running until I ran out of land, or life. Another part just wanted a drink.

Juan walked silently beside me through the dark. I felt a need to speak into the silence, but words would not come. Tears pooled in my eyes, but refused to fall. In the end I bent into the wind and walked on toward the flickering lights.

About the Author

Photo by Michael Gibson

Chris Helvey's short stories and poems have appeared in numerous magazines and journals, including *Kentucky Monthly*, *Idiolect*, *Kudzu*, *Nougat*, *The Chaffin Journal*, *Ace Weekly*, *Kentucky Blue*, *Modern Mountain Magazine*, *Best New Writing*, *New Southerner*, *Solstice*, *Bayou*, *Dos Passos Review*, and *Minnetonka Review*.

His chapbook *On The Boulevard* was released in 2011 by Finishing Line Press. He is a graduate of the Spalding University MFA in Writing program and currently serves as a writing coach and as editor of *Trajectory Journal*. He lives and writes in Frankfort, Kentucky with his wife Gina.

www.helveypress.com